Praise for the Night

Two Titles in
"Best 101 Romance Novels of the Last 10 years"
– Booklist

"Top 10 Romance of 2012."
– Booklist, *The Night Is Mine*

"Top 5 Romance of 2012."
–NPR, *I Own the Dawn*

"Suzanne Brockmann fans will love this."
–Booklist, *Wait Until Dark*

"Best 5 Romance of 2013."
–Barnes & Noble, *Take Over at Midnight*

"Nominee for Reviewer's Choice Award
for Best Romantic Suspense of 2014."
–RT Book Reviews, *Light Up the Night*

"Score 5 – Reviewer Top Pick – Buchman writes
with unusual sensitivity and delicacy for such a
hard-edged genre."
–Publishers Weekly, *Bring On the Dusk*

The Night Stalkers

Christmas at

Peleliu Cove

by

M. L. Buchman

Discover more by this author at:
www.mlbuchman.com

Cover images:
Interracial Couple with Roses © Keramsay | Dreamstime.com
A young and sexy brunette woman on a foggy background
© Maksim Shmeljov | Dreamstime.com
130826-A-AU838-003 (Chinook Helicopter)
© USASOC News Service | Flickr (cc)
"LCAC" © U.S. Navy photo by Photographer's Mate Airman
Sarah E. Ard | Wikimedia (cc)
Red and Green Candy cane over white
© Lucie Lang | Dreamstime.com (back cover)

Buchman Bookworks

Other works by M. L. Buchman:

Chapter 1

S*triding up the wide* steel bow ramp of the LCAC hovercraft, Petty Officer Nika Maier patted the ugly beast on its big black numbers—316—painted on the Navy-gray hull.

"Morning, baby." It was 1800 hours, an hour past sunset in the southern Mediterranean, the start of their day. Ever since the Night Stalkers had come to fly helicopters off their ship, operations had been done in a flipped-clock world of night. Even in their second year aboard, she really wasn't used to sleeping through the day, but that choice was made way above the pay grade of a Navy enlisted woman. Despite the warm December evening, there was a familiar damp air-and-steel chill down in the bowels of the USS *Peleliu* where Landing Craft Air Cushion 316 was typically parked.

"You got a soft spot in you," Chief Petty Officer Sly Stowell's deep voice echoed about the steel cavern that was the sea-level Well Deck of the ship. The *Peleliu's* massive stern ramp was currently raised, blocking out both the sea and the last of the sunset. In the shadows of the worklights she hadn't spotted him.

The Craftmaster was perched in the window of the hovercraft's starboard two-story control station, but after four years aboard his craft and four tours in the Navy, she'd lost her the ability to be surprised and simply waved a greeting.

"Only before a mission," she looked up at him. "Other than that…"

"…hard as steel," he finished for her. "In a mood to go kick some ass, Petty Officer Maier?" He offered his ritual start-of-shift greeting.

"Two boots better than one, Chief Stowell," her ritual reply before she climbed up into her Loadmaster's portside tower to prep the hovercraft. Even on days with no mission or exercise planned, they always made sure their craft was completely ready.

Sly dropped down the ladder and headed off to the evening briefing as she started checking over the LCAC—spoken like you were about to throw up—El-Cack! Some part of her warped Lower East Side Jewish sense of humor laughed every single time she heard it…or even thought it. The LCAC was homely as a New York bum, and so powerful that riding in it felt like an outing in the Lord's personal chariot. The juxtaposition got her every time. Probably made her completely sophomoric, but since no one could hear inside her head she figured no harm—no foul.

The portside lookout on Sly Stowell's hovercraft had become Petty Officer Nika Maier's favorite assignment since joining the Navy eight years before. In just another month she'd have been four years on old Lady 316.

Her first tour had been aboard the USS *George H. W. Bush*—then on its own first tour—but a girl could get totally lost in the five-thousand person city that was a newly commissioned aircraft carrier. The largest ship afloat in any navy, and still the crowd was worse than Times Square on New Year's Eve. She'd been a "red"—a red-vested serviceperson—in charge of loading and securing aircraft weapons and munitions systems. She was no aviator, but eventually grew sick of watching others burn into the sky on the hottest rides while she stood on the deck, ate exhaust fumes, and wished she was someone else.

For a brief time, a very brief time, the length of a two-week training run, she'd switched over to a Cyclone-class patrol boat without an aircraft in sight—not even a helipad. The hundred-and-eighty foot boat got in close to the action, mostly on security patrols for bigger ships. She'd enjoyed that. And the weapon systems were exceptional—there were six major weapon systems on a boat commonly crewed by just thirty men and women.

But that was the catch. On the USS *Firebolt*, a girl *couldn't* get lost. With such a small crew, the pickings were painfully thin for friendships, never mind any other thoughts. And the *Firebolt's* grapevine news network offered no privacy at all—you couldn't switch from drinking ice tea to lemonade at lunch without raising comments and questions. Good people, just way too far into your life.

Nika's Loadmaster checklist on the LCAC was short until they had a load. It was still fifteen minutes to start of shift, so she grabbed Jerome's checklist and began the mechanical inspection. She was the only one other than Sly who had cross-trained in all five of the crew positions; but it required constant practice to keep her skills fresh. Step one: Perimeter inspection. She headed down the bow ramp and began working her way along the spray skirt looking for untoward damage. The vague slit of light coming in over the *Peleliu's* rear ramp was no help at all, but the big worklights shone down. She pulled a flashlight out of her thigh pocket to double-check in the shadows cast by the overheads.

This, her third ship—three hundred feet shorter and half the personnel of the super carrier—landed right in the sweet spot. The USS *Peleliu* had serviced a Marine Expeditionary Unit for thirty-five years. Cobra helicopters and Harrier jets up on the flattop deck. Beneath that and the Hanger Deck were several decks carrying fifteen hundred gung-ho Marines and a third that many Navy to run the eight-hundred foot ship.

Even though Nika had liked the size, she'd still felt disconnected. Most of her second tour had gone by and she'd been doubting the point of re-upping for a third.

Then, four years ago, Sly had introduced her to heaven. She patted her baby-girl 316 again as she inspected the rear ramp gasket seal. She remembered the day with crystal clarity—

It had been midday and the Indian Ocean heat had dehydrated her to the point of weaving, weighed down by her bright red fire-resistant gear. She'd just left the Flight Deck after double-checking the Zuni missile control connections on yet another SuperCobra helicopter when Chief Petty Officer Sly Stowell had pulled her aside. Everyone knew Sly, he was just one of *those* guys. Super competent. There were days it seemed the *Peleliu* would sink without him aboard. Other times people said that they didn't need a command structure as long as Sly was around.

"You look bored as hammered shit, Maier," were the first words he'd ever spoken directly to her. She hadn't realized that he even knew her name.

Sometimes you answered honesty with honesty.

"Damn straight, Chief. If I never have to load another Hydra 70 missile tube, I'll die a happy woman."

"Good, come with me," and he'd walked away from her.

At a loss for what else to do, she'd grabbed a water bottle and staggered after him.

He'd led her down past the personnel decks. Even below the on-board Garage Decks filled with tanks, Humvees, and a dozen different land and amphibious vehicles. They were packed in so tightly that drivers used the roof hatches to get in and out of them once they were parked because they were jammed into the ship's lower holds door to door.

He led her down to the Well Deck. She hadn't been down here but once or twice since her on-boarding orientation tour two years before. The air had been oddly fresher than up on the exposed burning plain of the Flight Deck, and thanks be to the Lord our God.

Right at sea-level, the *Peleliu* sported a massive stern gate. When lowered into the water it formed an angled steel beach, opening the Well Deck directly to the sea. A variety of landing craft could be parked there.

"Meet my baby," Sly had sounded like a proud papa despite being from North Carolina rather than a good Jewish family. Or even a bad one like hers.

It was an LCAC, about the ugliest sea craft ever built. No surprise that they named the craft so that it sounded like a cat choking up a hairball. Worse, its only name was the black numbers painted as tall as Nika's torso. Aircraft, ships, even sailboats had names; El-Cacks didn't even rate that.

A Landing Craft Air Cushion was a ninety-foot-long by fifty-foot-wide rectangular platform with four jet engines down the sides—combined, they packed the same power as a Boeing 737 airliner. She sported two huge fans at the stern and two more that drove air underneath her big rubber skirt. There was a two-story control station at the starboard front corner for three people and a smaller tower for some loner to port. After the mayhem of the Flight Deck, that isolated tower had looked attractive.

At the base of either tower was a narrow cabin for a total of thirty troops. Behind them, on each side, were two big gas turbine jet engines and then the two massive rear fans. Down the center was the broad deck that could hold an M1A1 Abrams Main Battle Tank or a dozen armored Humvees parked in three tight lanes.

She finished rounding the craft doing her start of day inspection and looked up at it. Four years later, she still liked the look of it. Every now and then someone would tease her about being the "fair maiden locked in a tower." They didn't understand that from up there she could watch the world go by and not have to worry that her every thought conformed to some unwritten set of her mother's rules. Given the choice, she'd lock the door so that they could never drag her away.

Even on that first day aboard four years ago, she'd felt a strange affinity for the poor beast of a machine. Neither boat nor aircraft, the hovercraft lay there on the Well Deck like a stuck pig with her rubber skirt deflated and the front and rear ramps laying open on the rough wood of the presently dry Well Deck. The LCAC looked like someone had slashed open either end of a giant steel shoebox and pushed the end flaps down.

Nika had left the Flight Deck in broad daylight and fresh sea air—liberally laced with the kerosene bite of fresh-burned Jet-A fuel and echoing with the roar of turboshaft engines. The bowels of the ship were dark and quiet except for the beat of the sea against the outside of the hull and the low thrum of the big steam turbines directly below—more felt through the heels of her boots than heard. With the *Peleliu's* stern gate up, only a narrow slice of light entered above the gate. Big worklights did little to chase away the shadowed cave that was the Well Deck. It was like a man-cave on steroids—without the bar and big-screen television.

"Ain't she a beauty?" Sly had asked in his lazy Southern drawl, which echoed about the vast compartment like a whisper in Temple Emanu-el, the massive synagogue that her mother always dragged her to for the high holidays. As if showing up ten times a year somehow made them Upper East Side New York Jews rather than the last of the Lower East Side holdouts against the encroaching Chinatown. Encroaching, hell. The Chinese had overrun the old Jewish neighborhood and most of Little Italy…but the Maiers would not be nudged loose from their appointed place in the world.

Thankfully Sly didn't wait for her to answer.

"She needs a crew of five to fly and I just lost my portside spotter and Loadmaster," he aimed a nod up at the slim one-person tower that she'd liked on first sight. "Something about falling in love with an accountant, wants kids. You want kids, Maier?"

"Not yet, Chief. Haven't found a man worth having them with."

"Good. You already have your boatswain's rating. Welcome aboard."

And just that simply she'd been transferred to the LCAC crew—so fast that Sly might have sent in the paperwork before she'd ever descended the ladders and ramps to view her new posting. Her new world. The first part of her job was as weapons specialist to their pair of M2 .50 cal machine guns. Bit of a letdown from Harrier jets' and SuperCobra helicopters' vast array of heavy armament, but for the first time in her service, one of the machine guns was exclusively hers to control.

Also, he'd tempted her with the word "fly," because that's what an LCAC did—mere feet above the water but it flew.

Then Chief Stowell had followed up rapidly with Loadmaster training, assistant navigator, understudy engineer, and for her fourth tour he'd offered to start her on Craftmaster training, his own gig.

She'd re-upped.

And Sly was of course as good as his word, one of the main reasons she'd stuck with him for four years now. Men who weren't trying to sell a girl something were an unusual commodity in her experience, in or out of the service. Sly didn't sell anything. He actually believed. He was a lifer and was slowly convincing her that was a good thing. For lack of any clearer plan, she was starting to buy in.

Then right after she'd re-upped, the Marines had abandoned the *Peleliu* and tossed her toward the scrap heap. The Navy crew that ran her had gone into a deep tailspin of ugly funk. The band would be split up and scattered across the Navy. All of the newer personnel were indeed gone within days of the Marines' departure until under a quarter of her normal Navy crew remained. All of them who remained were old hands, not one below a rank of Petty Officer Second Class. Everyone assumed it was to oversee the decommissioning.

"Weirdest thing I've ever seen," Sly had mused quietly when the others had shipped out. "This is about the finest crew I've ever seen left aboard a doomed boat." They didn't have to wait long to find out why.

Just a few days later, in the dark of a long night the Night Stalkers of the US Army's 160th Special Operation Aviation Regiment 5th Battalion D Company had whispered aboard. With a full load, the *Peleliu* could carry thirty aircraft, the Night Stalkers brought seven.

But *whispered* was the operative word. Most of the 5D's helos were stealth-rigged, which Nika hadn't known existed outside of the raid on bin Laden's compound.

Instead of fifteen hundred Marines, the aging *Peleliu* shipped aboard the Night Stalkers 5D, six Delta operators, and thirty Special Operations grunts from the 75th Rangers. Since that night, the laughably small team had led them from crisis to crisis throughout Africa and the Middle East in a whirlwind which still wasn't showing any sign of easing. She'd seen more action in the eighteen months since their arrival than in her first six years in the Navy combined.

Her decision to join Sly's team—of which she was still the newest member even after four years—had been the best of her life. A close second had been dodging Mom's attempt to marry her off to Brian, *soon to be Doctor, honey,* Goldman. She'd have been better off with his younger brother Richie, a sweet geek, rather than that arrogant son of a bitch. Richie had eventually gone military and she'd lost track of him, not that it really mattered. Out of a million active soldiers in the US Armed Services she hadn't run into him or any other person she'd known back in the neighborhood—definitely her idea of good fortune.

Still no sign of Sly returning from the evening briefing by the time the other three of the LCAC crew arrived from "breakfast" just as the last of the sunset's glow disappeared above the stern gate. She didn't mention that she'd already done all three of their inspections; just enjoyed that they didn't find a single thing to do on their rounds. They were soon gathered in a line at the head of the bow ramp. Nothing happened.

"Five gets you a hundred we're on our butts again today," Tom Trambley, the craft's Navigator, grumbled.

"Maybe if you weren't such a shrimp, they wouldn't underestimate us so much and we'd draw more missions," Dave Newcomb, the craft's Engineer, looked down at his best friend. At six foot four of gangly North Dakotan, Dave was the tallest member of their crew, and the only one who could refer to Tom's six-three as short. Nika's five-six still left her a head shorter than any of them.

Jerome Walker, the Deck Mechanic and Assistant Loadmaster, typically didn't say a word.

"Maybe if you were shorter," Tom glared up at Dave, "you wouldn't make us look so damn ridiculous. Jerome, you're gonna have to cut us a hole in the control cabin roof just for Dave's swollen ego. Course he spent all that height growing his head, means his pecker is the size of a bean."

"You'd know," Nika was feeling good so she joined in the fray. The Chief's evening mission briefing was running too long for an exercise.

Jerome's snort of laughter was as much as he ever said unless something was broken or some grunt didn't park their vehicle exactly as he directed—he was the LCAC's other Loadmaster. When that happened his Georgia came out thick and biting. No Marine or Ranger made that mistake again if they could help it.

A clatter of steps on the ramp down from the Garage Deck cut off Tom's sputtering response. They all recognized Sly's confident stride, but there were more people behind him; a guaranteed conversation stopper.

Yep! Nika kept the thought to herself about getting the last word. *Timing was everything.*

Tom was such an easy target that teasing him wasn't really fair, not that it stopped her of course. He was the only one of them other than Sly who sported a wedding ring. He had a wife and kid back home and almost never shut up about them—proud dad didn't begin to cover it. Way too easy a target.

Sly had hooked up with the ship's Chief Steward last Christmas; hooked up permanently right down to the ring and a white wedding ashore with family and the whole nine yards. Nika had been invited and had worn her formal dinner-dress whites—with the slacks option. She didn't even own the skirt option for her dress whites and absolutely not a damned gown. She'd sworn off dresses as soon as she'd grown old enough to face down her mother. And a wedding dress? Never gonna happen, even if Gail now-Stowell had looked completely amazing in hers.

"Make 'er ready," Sly's call echoed down the ramp before he made the last turn into view at the head of the Well Deck. It was the same words he used to start every live mission. A training exercise started, "Let's go prove we still know how."

"Way ahead of you, Chief," Nika replied as he swung into view at a quick stride. Then she couldn't resist, "Had it all inspected and prepped before any of these jokers even showed up."

"What?" Tom exclaimed and Dave just looked bummed. Jerome nodded as if to say, "Of course you did."

She heard the distant sound of several small engines coughing to life up in the garages and her pulse picked up its pace. "What kind of heat are we packing tonight?" She and Jerome had to make sure that any vehicles were positioned so that the LCAC's loading was properly balanced and she'd fly true.

"Lots of little heat, Petty Officer Maier," a deep voice wrapped in a soft Southern deeper and richer than Sly's called out from the head of the loading ramp. "Fast and dirty heat. And a pair of RSOVs just in case." Ranger Spec Ops Vehicles—they absolutely confirmed there was action tonight.

Nika glanced up the ramp to see Lieutenant Clint Barstowe arrive close behind Sly. The commander of the 75th Rangers platoon was a big man, and loaded for bear. Combat uniform, armored vest, and enough magazines for his rifle to take out an entire platoon of bad guys himself. He looked incredible. Not *overly* handsome, just damned good looking. Strong shoulders on a powerful frame. But mostly he radiated power—dark and dangerous. It wasn't that you didn't want to meet him in a trashy alley; even in broad daylight you'd best pray he was on your side.

His helmet was snagged on his belt, hooked over the butt of his knife. His service piece holstered on the other hip and a rifle over his shoulder.

Then he totally spoiled the pretty picture by wearing a red Santa hat complete with white fur trim and pom-pom perched atop his Ranger-short black hair.

#

"Need to grow a white beard if you're planning to live up to that hat, Lieutenant. Besides, you're a little early there. And aren't you from Arkansas? Do they even have Christmas that far south?"

Clint grinned at the heckler in surprise. Maier was always teasing people, but it was the first time she'd aimed a jibe at him in the eighteen months he'd been aboard.

"You snickering at my festive fedora, Petty Officer Nika Maier? Thanksgiving is a week gone; it's December now. Where's your Christmas spirit, Petty Officer?"

"I'm Jewish, Lieutenant. And we're in the Southern Mediterranean where it's seventy-eight Fahrenheit."

"And you're using that as an excuse *not* to be merry?"

"As I said, sir, Jewish. Against our religion to be merry because we don't need an excuse to feel someone is out to get us—we already know they are. Besides, that's not a fedora without a brim and an indented crown." She picked up a three-foot steel pry bar used for tightening the vehicle tie-down chains and waved it at him, revealing a surprising strength in her slender frame. "Be glad to fix the latter problem for you," her cheerful tone completely belied her prior declaration regarding merriness.

"And you never had a Christmas tree? I can only pity the poor, neglected child."

"Might have had a Hanukkah bush, sir. Might have had pretty lights on it. Maybe even presents that were opened on December 25th. But I promise, I wasn't merry about it."

Damn but he liked her. Nika Maier had sass and a slow smile that was hard to tease out, but it was definitely worth the effort. And she always gave a hundred percent just like a Ranger and it was easy to respect that, even if she was a Navy swabbie. More Navy swabbies looked like her and he just might change branches of the service.

"My beard comes in as black as my hair, ma'am. Black as my mama's." Lena Barstowe was still acclaimed as a beautiful woman even in her fifties. And able to stare down the entire board of the Little Rock hospital she ran if she didn't like one of their decisions.

"A mama's boy. I should have known."

"Not the way you mean it, but yes. Hundred percent! Hoo-ah!" She come up the hard way, nurse to senior administrator—doing a whole lot to respect. Raising he and his little sister on her own, she'd been both warm and strict. And he'd do anything to protect them both.

"So you're a lump of coal Santa. Wouldn't want to find you in my stocking; could ruin a whole Hanukkah Bush day. And *Ma'am?* Do I look like a ma'am?"

Nika Maier looked like a lot of good things he wouldn't mind finding in stockings and a Ms. Claus mini-dress—an image he decided to keep to himself, especially because she hadn't set aside that steel bar yet. Clint went for a different conversation though the image didn't exactly fade away.

"Can't say I much like sleighs either. Especially y'alls air cart," he did his best to make the last a dismissive sneer, as beneath a gentleman soldier of Little Rock.

Maier brandished her pry bar again, proving the correctness of his earlier decision on keeping certain things to himself. "You take that back, Army. Nobody insults our little girl 316 and gets away with it."

Clint heard the first engine idling down the ramp behind him and used it as an excuse to shift aside out of the main line of Maier's fire, raising his hands in mock defeat. Even idling, the engines rang about the space loudly enough for him to pull on a set of heavy earmuffs. The big fans to clear the exhaust fumes out of the ship had also roared to life, making conversation impossible. Claiming the final word—or at least gesture—Maier offered a final wave of her weapon before moving to load the craft.

Lamar and Jeffries backed the two RSOVs down the Well Deck's ramp and up the LCAC's. The Ranger Special Operations Vehicles were Land Rovers on steroids. Like the old Korean and Vietnam War Jeeps, they had no doors to delay exit or attack. They carried seven Rangers, mounted a pair of heavy machine guns—an M240 and an M2—and were nearly indestructible. Everything a growing boy wanted when riding into a shit storm.

Nika guided them into position without a single miscue. She'd already been a fixture when he pulled his first mission launching from the *Peleliu*. Just watching her had done a lot to shift his thinking about women in the military. She was five-six, just a slip of a thing with shaggy brunette hair that tended to ruffle in the slightest breeze. Half of the time she looked as if she should be teaching besotted kindergarteners.

Instead, she was completely at home in a heavy-duty war machine like the hovercraft. The other half of the time she reminded him of Natalie Portman in that *V for Vendetta* movie. He'd have to watch that again—he'd thought the movie merely okay the first time, but imagining Nika Maier in the lead role, especially after the heroine became a kickass warrior for truth and justice, might enhance his opinion a few hundred-fold.

After Nika and the silent Jerome chained down the RSOVs so that they wouldn't shift during transport, other Rangers began rolling down the ship's ramp and boarding the LCAC. Six on dirt bikes and four driving four-man MRZRs—rugged-ass all-terrain vehicles with a roll-cage and a swivel mounted M2 Browning on the passenger side. They were smaller and lighter, but just as tough as their RSOV big brothers.

"C'mon, you elves. Get aboard and get 'em pinned down. We're gonna hafta be waiting on the Navy as it is. Don't give them an excuse to be even slower."

He'd kept a weather eye on Maier who flicked a finger in his direction. At his laugh she called out.

"We been waiting on your sorry behinds half an hour, Lieutenant. 'Rangers Lead the Way' like hell." She didn't even break stride to insult him. Didn't quite offer that hot smile, but he could see her fighting it. Damn woman was a hoot.

Women usually didn't make him laugh much. His ex-wife sure as hell hadn't when she'd bailed after only two years. She'd vacuum cleaned his bank account on her way into the arms of a used car dealer while Clint had been overseas. She and Mr. Used Car had kept bleeding his Army pay out of the joint account for six months while he'd been in Afghanistan. The Bitch—only way he ever thought of her now—had thought that bleeding him until the last second was a better option than Dear John-ing him while Al-Qaeda had been trying to bleed him for real.

Of course his service brothers had gotten wind of it. Without his knowledge, one had cancelled Mr. Car's insurance policy. The rest of the squad had leveled the parking lot; seventy-eight cars good for nothing but the crusher. They'd looped the security cameras so that there were no gaps and no evidence. Never fuck with a Ranger.

He'd reamed them good about taking such actions, risking their careers that way, and wanted to thank every man Jack of them. They understood loyalty even if women didn't. As a bonus, after Mr. Car's *inexplicable* loss, the Bitch had dumped his ass and would have cleaned out his account too if his brothers hadn't already seen to that for both of them.

His team had offered to replace all the money she'd taken but he didn't want a single cent—it felt soiled by *her*. So, they'd donated the whole lump into the Special Operations Warrior Foundation. A lot of kids who'd lost their Spec Ops dads had gone to college in Mr. Car's name. Two years of Clint's income was gone, but it was helping kids, which reduced the sting. By pure dumb luck he'd never gotten around to adding her name to the retirement account that held the bulk of his savings, or she'd have stripped that too.

Nika Maier walked across his field of view on her way to double-check one of the tie-downs.

Shit! How had he gotten off into that ugly headspace again? He'd thought he was done with that. Bitch was gone and no other woman was coming in close ever again except for sport. Wouldn't mind sporting with Maier a bit, except she didn't strike him as that sort of woman. Too bad. Damn it! Still thinking dead-end shit.

"Move your asses!" Clint roared at the last of the Rangers jogging down the ramp as if it was their fault. He tried to soften it, "Time to bring a little Christmas cheer to the heathens."

He considered tonight's mission. Yeah, one terrorist camp going down extra hard. He definitely needed a little of that kind of rock 'n' roll right now.

"We will!..." He shouted out over the heads of the boarding troops.

"We will!…" He repeated the call.

"Wreck you!" Thirty US Rangers roared with a double-stomp of their boots on the LCAC's hard steel deck followed by a unison-shouted "Hoo-ah!" in place of the handclap of the altered Queen song. They picked it up as a double-time marching cadence.

"We will…we will…Wreck you!" Half of them singing.

The Well Deck roared with the echoes. They matched their beat to the echo's, making it all the louder.

Stomp! Stomp! "Hoo-ah!" Half keeping the chant.

Damn but he loved these guys.

Chapter 2

*N*ika's ears were still ringing from the Rangers' boarding
song. Even though they were now tucked away below in their
soundproofed cabins and she was up in her tower, it still seemed
to reverberate from the craft's steel hull itself.

Dave had fired off the LCAC's four big Vericor gas turbine
engines. Inside the Well Deck the roar was deafening. And that
was despite her full helmet and own sound-insulated tower
cabin. With her acknowledgement that they looked good from
her vantage point, Dave raised the ramps and inflated the skirt.

In an instant the cavernous Well Deck disappeared behind
a solid fog of spray. The high-speed windshield wipers had little
effect. The deck hadn't been flooded, which it could do for hulled
sea craft, but the big fans beneath the LCAC found every bit of
stray water and atomized it.

As Craftmaster, Sly lifted them six inches off the deck and
eased them backward toward the now open stern gate of the
Peleliu.

With a visceral shock they emerged from the brightly-lit interior of the Well Deck out onto the pitch black of the open ocean.

She pulled down her night-vision goggles and her view reemerged as soon as the spray could blow sideways. She had an unimpeded three-sixty vista. To her right, in the control station on the other front corner of the LCAC sat Dave and Tom with Sly at the outside. Jerome was below, ready to tackle any emergency. At the stern, beyond the chained-down vehicles, were the two massive driving fans. Off the port side was the faintest hint of the Tunisian coast, little more than a green glimmer of heat in the far distance.

Sly spun them clear from the *Peleliu* with the smooth twist of a dancer's pirouette.

Another of her mother's dreams, her daughter the ballerina dancing at Rockefeller Center. And yet another "disappointment to the family" as Nika never even made it to the lead in the recital at Mrs. Mandelbaum's Dance Studio. Nor the assistant lead. If Mom had let her take a martial art, there might have been something to see, but Nika had to wait for the Navy to learn anything useful like hand-to-hand combat. Still hadn't gotten a chance to study Kung Fu or Taekwondo, but they were on her to-do list.

In moments, the massive wall of the *Peleliu's* looming hull passed astern.

"Planning to tell us anytime soon what we're doing tonight, Chief?" Nika called over the intercom. "I'm guessing we're not just joyriding thirty of the Army's finest out for a sightseeing cruise along the Tunisian beaches."

"You asking me for a mission brief, Maier? What happened to trust? And faith in your commander?"

"You've been hanging out with Lieutenant Barstowe too much, Chief." Not a surprise. Clint Barstowe had stood as best man at Sly's wedding, with Delta Force Colonel Michael Gibson as his second. She hadn't really been thinking about it at the time, but the Lieutenant had looked damned fine in his dress blues. "He gives you an inflated sense of self worth."

"Hey, I'm busy driving here."

"Glad to show you how that's supposed to be done at any time, Chief." And boy oh boy would she. She'd gone through Craftmaster training and Nika flew every chance Sly afforded her. But he was still the LCAC's Craftmaster and the *Peleliu* only carried the one. The Navy had offered her an LCAC on another ship, but she'd turned them down cold before she could even think about it. She wanted to fly, but she wanted to stay with this crew and this ship even more.

The hovercraft was the perfect mix between watercraft and aircraft—three feet up and able to move like a bat out of hell. Handling was also as dicey as an aircraft that was permanently caught in that instant just after takeoff or seconds before landing with no long break of "cruise at altitude" perks included.

"I'm with Maier on this one, Sly," Clint Barstowe's voice sounded from the passenger cabin below. "After all, she called us the Army's finest."

She'd forgotten that the Ranger commander would be on the intercom system to monitor operations. Normally he was dead silent, but he was always on the system somewhere, following status reports until it was time to rush the beach.

"You misheard, Lieutenant. Must have been some noise on the line. Aren't the Rangers known as the military's *laziest* far and wide?"

"Only if you don't count the Navy, Maier. Besides, Sly," he continued, "she's way prettier than you are."

The bitter taste of remembered rage welled up in her throat and lashed out before she could stop it.

"Go to hell, Lieutenant! How I got here has shit to do with how I look." The fire wrenched in her gut, but she should never have let it loose like that. Her mother's "But you're so pretty, dear" answer to every one of Nika's aspirations and failures. Especially the failures to marry. The age when

Jewish daughters sold themselves to successful doctors with "pretty" as their main attribute was generations gone…and everyone except Mom knew that. The final fight had been over her signing up for the Navy, "But why would a girl as pretty as you do that? It will ruin your looks and then no one will ever want to marry you."

There was an uncomfortable silence on the intercom.

"Sorry," the Lieutenant said it softly, sounding far more contrite than should be possible for six feet of US Ranger.

She tried to answer that it didn't matter, but it did and she'd sworn off lying-to-appease long ago. Instead she kept her silence. No one made a sound until Nika thought the storm of the LCAC's engine roar was going to break over her like a tidal wave.

Sly finally broke the silence—as if there hadn't been any. Yet another reason she appreciated her boss. "*Peleliu* is fifty miles offshore Tunisia. We're going to slide in on coastal waters with the government's permission for a training exercise. We'll be taking the C203 highway inland. Fifty kilometers south we'll *disappear* out of Tunisian territory."

"That's…" Nika tried to picture the maps of the area. "That's central nowhere. Are there even roads?" She knew it was a mistake as soon as she said it.

"Roads?" Sly asked, imitating the mad Doc Brown in his favorite movie, *Back to the Future*. "Where we're going, we don't need roads!"—the only line he ever quoted.

"Let me guess, there aren't any."

Barstowe chuckled—had to be him, she'd recognize anyone else's—but he was smart enough to keep his mouth shut. Yeah, *that* she'd have to apologize for. It did matter, but she shouldn't have tromped on him.

"Only at the outset," Sly admitted cheerfully. "The C203 is a dirt and gravel highway that slides right down the Tunisia-Libya border. That gets us part way. There's a terrorist camp in the Libyan desert that will never expect an attack from the deep desert to their south."

As long as there were no surprise obstacles over three feet tall, theirs was about the only US military craft that could cross the terrain. A tank could, but only with four people and at forty miles an hour, not nearly eighty with a full load like the hovercraft.

"Bad ass bunch of boys," Barstowe sounded suddenly angry, his voice that had been so contrite earlier abruptly harsh. A clear reminder that he was the commander of a platoon of very lethal Army Rangers. "They've twisted their religion so out of shape that they think prisoners are a right granted by God, especially young female ones. They've taken a lesson from the Boko Haram bastards to the south."

Her world fuzzed out of focus.

Nika tried to breathe, but couldn't seem to find any air. Somehow she'd dodged that particular hell. But she knew a lot of girls who hadn't. Keila, her best friend in high school, had been gang-raped during freshman year at college. It had started as some drunken party game, landed her in the hospital with operations that had to cut out any chance of family she'd always wanted so much, and ended with a bullet in her brain.

Perpetrators brought to justice, zero.

Keila had always been the shining star: A-student, engineering, Navy ROTC, going somewhere. Nika had been a purposeless drifter scraping Cs on an English degree she'd never use. Keila had also been Nika's refuge. In high school, if she was with Keila, everyone left her alone. And in the last few years, as her mother grew crazier and her dad quieter—if that was even possible—Nika had visited so much that she'd practically lived with Keila's family.

After the funeral Nika had skipped the wake, dropped out of school, and signed up Navy that very day.

Tonight was going to be different. Tonight would be payback and damn the soul of every man in that camp to hell.

"Landfall in three," Tom announced, his voice unusually businesslike.

Deep breath. Another. On the third, her thoughts cleared enough to recall this was a mission. On the fourth enough that she could see again.

A glance at the mission clock. She'd only blanked for seconds, but the cesspool of her past had washed over her. She needed a shower to wash away the feelings that always accompanied her helpless rage.

Focus! Just goddamn focus!

No surprises on her dashboard of instruments. A careful inspection out her window showed no vehicles broken loose on the deck—not that such a problem was likely, especially in such mild seas.

Nika rubbed her face and strained her vision ahead, but there was little to see. Radar said no ships in the area, not even any pleasure craft. The beach was dark except for a brightly lit ship's terminal for offloading oil tankers about ten kilometers to the west. It was little more than a distant twinkle.

With a skill she could only admire, Sly took the beach without slowing down. The wide cloud of water spray that shot in every direction from beneath the racing LCAC was replaced by a swath of sand particles. She shut off the windshield wipers to avoid grinding the sand into the glass.

They crested the berm in a half ski jump—half wave roll that left them bobbing back and forth as they raced southward.

From experience Nika knew they were leaving a rooster tail of dust to float behind them in a long choking line. It might not settle for an hour or more. They were now the roadrunner leaving a visible dust trail for Wiley E. Coyote to chase. Except they were the ones on the attack.

The C203 highway was brightly lit by the infrared searchlights that the LCAC shone ahead. In her NVGs, night-vision goggles, everything was in shades of green from the near black of fire bush and sand to the middle green strip of the wide gravel road stretching ahead, still holding the December warmth. Two thin stripes of lighter green showed where a vehicle had passed in the last hour or so, leaving a path heated by friction, of the tires compacting gravel. Dual tires; a bus or truck.

The LCAC was the width of the entire two lane road plus the shoulders. Without NVGs their vehicle was pitch black, moving at eighty miles an hour, and noisy as a jetliner with a bad attitude.

"Chariot of justice."

"You got that straight, lady."

She hadn't realized she'd spoken aloud until Barstowe agreed with her. She could still hear the hint of apology in the care he was taking with how he said it.

"You want to get square with me, Ranger?"

"Just show me the way, Navy."

"You go out there tonight and you kick some serious ass."

"Deal!"

# # #

There was an edge in Nika's voice. It went beyond this mission, took a right turn at pissed, and detoured straight into barely-controlled rage. Do not pass Go. Do not collect two hundred dollars.

Clint recognized it. When a Ranger had watched one too many buddies go down, you couldn't miss it. It happened when the forward operating base was too far forward and was no longer operating so well. Then it became a base of mixed despair and terror. Ultimately, unable to do anything but defend the base, rage tipped free and spilled out the business end of a rifle. Ammunition flew so thick it could darken the skies in those moments.

And it was always a mistake. It achieved little and always created a massive letdown. It burned ammo and anger until it was like a drug you couldn't let go of. He'd lost too many good men to that rage.

He was surprised to hear it fully embodied in the slip of a woman that was Petty Officer Nika Maier. He was also now worried. She was only partly in control of the hovercraft that was supposed to deliver him and his team. That kind of anger made a soldier unpredictable, capable of Herculean feats but also stupid ones. Squadmates had clambered atop HESCO barrier walls of stone and earth, clear of any defense, and screamed in rage at their heavily armed enemies. When their bloody bodies were blown backward on top of their comrades, no one spoke of it.

Your son fell protecting his squad…freeing hostages…saving a fallen comrade's life.

Never: *He died because The Rage won and he lost.*

Nika Maier had The Rage. He could hear it gut deep and ocean wide.

Clint didn't know whether to pity her or try to help; steering clear didn't appear to be an option. Sly had said that she had more potential than any sailor he'd ever known aboard the *Peleliu*. He hadn't said that she might not survive all that potential.

Maybe Sly hadn't seen it.

It took facing death, not just in some litter dragged off a helicopter, but in its ugliest, messiest form to feel The Rage at that level.

He studied the men sitting with him. Rather than sitting up with Sly, he was down in the troop cabin and had picked up an intercom headset there. Despite earplugs and sound insulation, the cabin echoed with the gas turbine engines' roar. They were packed in tighter than bark on a tree. Half of these men had been with him in Afghanistan. Every one of them had seen two or more tours in the Dustbowl. Since then they'd flown as embedded trainers and action support throughout the region. And that was before they'd mounted up on the *Peleliu*.

Clint knew the measure of every one of these men. Knew how they'd behave under fire, when desperately bored, when delivering humanitarian aid during earthquake relief efforts.

What did he really know about the Navy crew? He and Sly had grown close since the Rangers and Night Stalkers had come aboard—the easy friendship between two career enlisted men. Even if Clint had gone officer, he still thought of himself by his enlisted roots. The day Sly had asked him to stand best man at his wedding had surprised the hell out of Clint. And touched him deeply. Too bad he'd never be able to return the honor.

The other guys on the LCAC crew had seemed steady and reliable enough.

But Maier had always stood out.

Clint knew the type; he'd seen it among his own teams often enough. Someone who just didn't fit. They could be skilled, committed, dead reliable, but they remained an outsider. It didn't make them less of a soldier but it did make them less predictable—a constant crack in a team's cohesiveness.

That's why he'd sided on the "no female Rangers" side of the debate. Not because he had a thing against them; hell, if they could make it through Ranger School, Airborne, SERE, and RASP there was no question about their qualifications. He wasn't like the other idiots who thought they were somehow skating through or less qualified even if they did make it.

But he didn't like that "crack" in his teams. When he'd been asked to form up a platoon in support of a long-term combined Night Stalkers and Delta Force operation, he'd selected his men very carefully. Rangers were all smart and tough, but he'd been careful to quietly shed the outsider types and definitely those who had The Rage.

And now he was doubting Petty Officer Maier seated just up the ladder his shoulder was pressed against. He shrugged against his vest's straps trying to loosen the itch that had lodged there. A dozen years of service had taught him to listen to that itch, but that didn't mean he had to like what it was telling him.

#

They settled LCAC-316 five miles and three minutes south of the Libyan camp. Nika knew that under Gaddafi, terrorists had done well here. Now that there was no consolidated government at all, they thrived. Al-Qaeda, Libya Shield Force, Ansar al-Sharia—it didn't matter. They all needed to be erased.

Nika was down the ladder even before the skirt was deflated. The engines were still whistling down from full roar toward idle; they'd be keeping the LCAC ready for immediate flight.

It took her and Jerome less than two minutes to crack loose the chains on all of the vehicles. Dave had the skirt deflated and the front ramp already lowered to the arid sand amid a swirl of choking dust.

The Rangers had saddled up. The two big Ranger Special Operations Vehicles rolled down the ramp and onto the sand. Dark clumps of struggling growth showed black in her NVGs against the background of warm earth still radiating the day's heat. Once the RSOVs were clear, a swirling cloud of smaller MRZR off-road vehicles and dirt bikes followed after. Without his Santa hat to distinguish him, she'd missed seeing Clint Barstowe roll out.

She wished she'd had a chance to apologize. Not for voicing her irritation—well, maybe a little—but definitely for unloading her mother's shit on his head.

But she knew from experience that Lieutenant Barstowe led from the front and he'd be out in the lead MRZR. She watched the departing Rangers as long as she could. They climbed a low dune and then they were gone except for the faint trail of heat from their passage across her night vision.

"You okay, Nika?"

"More pissed at myself than anything else, Jerome." The two of them stood alone at the head of the ramp.

"Uh-huh," his grunt was sympathetic. "Chains," he continued.

Nika turned to help Jerome reset the tie-down chains. They might not have the luxury of time when the Rangers reloaded and everything had to be ready.

It was only as they were laying out the last one that the double-meaning of Jerome's word caught up with her. What chains were still tying her down?

Crap! Jerome always was the deep one.

Chapter 3

Clint and four of his top shooters edged up behind the last clump of fire bush to look out at the camp. Terrence said that's what it was, just another withered creosote look-alike plant to him. They'd left the vehicles a mile back where they could be on site in ninety seconds. The desert had chilled during their hike in. It was now an hour to midnight, the darkness was thick and the puffs of their own breath showed up on the NVGs, even if it wasn't cold enough for them to make white vapor clouds. Have to breathe shallow and through their noses when they got in close in case they had any NVGs for their guards.

He'd wanted to ride into camp hell-bent and take them by surprise, but there were prisoners and hostages at risk. He had to secure as many of them as possible before the battle began.

There was no need to discuss tactics, the layout was obvious enough. Garbage-heap worthy tents for the new recruits. They wouldn't have any luxuries at all; hopefully not any live weapons either.

There were a half dozen trucks: four for transport, and two Toyota Highlanders with heavy machine guns mounted on the back—technicals. They were bad news, but Night Stalker Kara Moretti's drone overflight had spotted them already, so they weren't a surprise.

Mud-brick buildings lined the other side of the camp in a hodge-podge fashion that said this had once been a village. There was only one guard visible, and he was watching the third building on the left rather than the camp's perimeter.

Confirmed. Prisoners in number three on the left.

Posting a solo guard seemed sloppy, even for terrorists, but his attention confirmed that building was their target. A second man exited the doorway of the building next to that one, his rifle over his shoulder and his hands rearranging the lower part of his clothes. He came over to lean against the outside of the third building and waved for the other guard to go into the second; the man didn't hesitate.

Confirmed. Female sex slaves in number four on the left.

No other guards on the compound. Nice of them to show him so clearly where both the prisoners and the captured women were housed.

Two guards posted. Both dead men.

He pointed to Hanson and then the two technicals. Ruiz, Mitchum and Dupree followed him as they slipped up to the buildings. The guard still itching his crotch went down silently with a snapped neck. Ruiz and Mitchum eased quietly into the third building to free and guard the prisoners. In seconds, Ruiz was back and flashed five fingers, then two more. Seven hostages. Exactly the count they'd expected.

Clint stepped into the next doorway where he assumed the women were kept. The room was lit by a single guttering lantern, not that he needed it through his goggles. He saw a dozen women huddled against a wall. Some of them couldn't be old enough for high school, if these radical bastards had believed in educating women. On the far side of the room the guard who had entered the building still wore his rifle across his back. He had one of the girls bent over a table with her clothes pulled up around her waist and was a moment from driving himself into her.

It was a moment he never had a chance to enjoy.

Clint dropped a pair of silenced rounds into his head.

The guard's hands reflexively dug into the girl's hips and she whimpered in despair; then she yelped when he collapsed on top of her. Several of the women screamed in surprise, only now aware of him standing in the shadowed doorway.

"Well, so much for that." Clint keyed the radio, "Do it!"

He waved Dupree into the room and counted to three for Hanson's grenade launcher to fire across the compound.

At four seconds, two small explosions announced direct hits on the Toyota pickups.

At five, the second round of 40mm grenades landed and it was too much—the technicals blew apart with a massive roar that shook the air and filled the doorway with blinding light and a wall of dust and sand.

"Stay!" Clint shouted in Arabic to the shrieking women. He repeated it in French in case any of them had been taken from the countries to the south. He dragged the dead guard off the girl and shoved her toward the others.

Then he moved back to guard position as Dupree rapidly checked that the women were all unarmed. They were. Dupree fell back to guard and Clint shifted to the doorway to begin sniping at the armed men pouring into the compound.

Surveillance had said there were over a hundred men in this camp, far too many for he and his four teammates, not that it kept them from trying. Any man with a weapon went down hard.

But the Rangers weren't alone.

Thirty seconds after those first screams of panic had alerted the compound, an unholy sound lashed from the sky.

A pair of Night Stalker helicopters had flown a different route in from the *Peleliu*. They now made racing passes less than a hundred feet above the roofs. With each pass they unleashed five-second bursts from their M134 miniguns. As if an entire Ranger Battalion all shot their rifles every five seconds, four hundred rounds of hell unleashed like a dragon's angry roar—still one of the most terrifying sounds Clint had ever heard. It made his nuts clench just imagining what that could do if he got in their way. Lines of fire chewed across the compound in swirling arcs of tracer-green light that left no armed figure untouched.

At ninety seconds, right on schedule, the rest of his Rangers roared up to encircle the camp. The terrorists who bolted for the safety of the desert didn't find it.

In three minutes, the main battle was done.

The Rangers closed in and began room-to-room clearing. Firefights, brief ones, announced pockets of resistance.

By five minutes even that was done. Now only the occasional single shot echoed across the compound.

And then he heard it, the heavy drone, like a jetliner coming in to land. The massive LCAC crested that last dune where he'd crouched less than a dozen minutes ago. It nosed right into the compound, its big fans tumbling aside both bodies and debris, like a whale cresting through the ocean. Looking down at him from her high perch sat Nika Maier.

# # #

Despite being geared up like every other Ranger, Clint Barstowe was impossible to miss. He stood in the center of the mayhem of the fire-lit village square as if he was invincible. Men rushed by, crouched, weapons raised.

Clint stood tall, his rifle held loosely, as he surveyed the scene. Nika wondered how many rounds were in his magazine; far fewer than he started with she'd wager.

When someone hurried up to him, he directed them to new tasks with easy gestures and supreme confidence. He looked like one of those arrogant sons of bitches who thought they were indestructible.

He also looked like a dark god.

When his gaze turned in her direction, a shiver ran through her. She couldn't tell if it was warmth or a chill, but it was powerful enough that she checked to make sure that her hands weren't near anything critical.

After the last of the gunfire had ceased and he called an "All clear" over the radio, he tugged off his helmet. Then from his waistband, he pulled out his Santa hat and tugged it on. When he saluted her formally, despite the Rangers and prisoners swirling about him, she couldn't help but laugh.

The laugh was cut off when she saw the women staggering out of the building behind him.

Then the dark warrior god that was Lieutenant Clint Barstowe Army Ranger turned and began helping the women and girls as if that was the most important task in the world. When he entered the building and came out carrying a young woman who clung to him in desperate hope, he looked even better.

Nika really didn't want to see what he carried, but she couldn't stop watching him as he delivered his burden to the massive Chinook helicopter that had settled on the other side of the square and was loading survivors. She really didn't need Clint to turn out to be a completely decent guy.

# # #

"You ever going to talk to me again, Maier?" They were alone in the *Peleliu's* Well Deck. The mission was done and he'd hung around until all of the gear had been restowed. Now it was just the two of them still aboard the LCAC.

"Don't see why I would, Ranger." But the sass was back in Nika's voice which made Clint feel better. At the camp, she'd reloaded the Ranger's vehicles while he'd been securing the prisoners in one helo and the women and hostages in another. It was clear that if they put them together, the men wouldn't be reaching the *Peleliu* intact.

By the time he'd double-checked his Ranger head-count back aboard the LCAC, she'd already been up in her perch and busy with getting them safely out of the camp and out of Libya. The race back to the ship and then the trickiest operation an LCAC ever did, slipping inside the Well Deck to park safely once more in the *Peleliu's* belly, had kept her busy. Though he'd admired the precise clarity of the observations she'd given to Sly over the intercom to assist him.

He'd waited until she was done and they were the last two in the closed and red-lit Well Deck. The rest of his team would be in the showers or headed off to dinner.

Nika was just finishing up. Even now she was stowing the last of the tools, the three-foot pry bar she'd offered to use on his skull.

"You did promise to forgive me if I kicked some serious ass."

"Maybe. Maybe not," her tone was light as if she was a cat playing with a new toy. "I figure your guys did that for you. Far as I could see, you just stood around and called in the cavalry when it got messy. Not sure that counts for much, Army. Half forgiven at most," she dropped the bar into its cradle with a bang that rang sharply enough in the steel cavern to make him wince. She stepped up to stand close in front of him. Very close; he wouldn't have to reach far to discover how soft the skin of her cheek might be. He looked down into her deep brown eyes; almost too big for her face, they gave her an inviting openness. *Eyes are the windows to the soul?* Then Nika Maier had one plus-sized soul in that trim body.

"Way I see it, *Navy*," he riposted, "that makes us about equal. If I just moseyed around with my rifle and my Santa hat, then you sat back and let Sly do the driving. Pretty cozy berth there in your hovercraft sleigh."

She crossed her arms and tipped her head sideways as she continued to look up at him. It didn't quite hide the smile that started there.

"I really don't want to like you, Lieutenant Barstowe."

"That much I figured out on my own, Petty Officer Maier. Any particular reason?"

"Oh, I can come up with a bunch."

"This should be good. Want to explain some of them over chow?"

Her reluctant smile opened up. Damn it was a sparkler. She went from pretty, right through cute and damned cute, and over to amazing faster than her hovercraft raced over the open ocean on a calm day.

She made Clint temporarily forget about his self promise that he wasn't ever going to tangle with a woman again for longer than it took to sweat up some sheets. Nika Maier was a serious woman; made a man think serious thoughts even when he didn't want to.

"Okay, but you're going to have to do me a favor, Ranger."

"Another one?" Clint tried to sound put out despite feeling pretty pleased about this moment.

"Yes!" She shoved against the center of his chest hard enough that he had to step back. "Go shower first. You stink! See you in fifteen minutes."

Then she turned and walked away down the LCAC's ramp and up the Well Deck's. It wasn't some loose-hipped, teasing, woman's walk, but it still jolted his system as if it was just that.

Shower. Cold one. Been a long time since he'd thought of the need for one of those.

Chapter 4

The Mess Hall was mayhem. When the Marine Expeditionary Unit had been aboard, the ship had been packed to the limits of her welded seams. Officers Mess was forward on the 02 Deck. Chiefs Mess directly below. The Seamen and the two Marine Messes were to the stern. With the MEU aboard, every sailor knew her place.

That was all changed now and Nika missed it. With the departure of the MEU, the Navy contingent had also been cut in half and a bit more. Without dozens of aircraft aboard, far fewer Flight Deck and service personnel were required. Without fifteen hundred Marines underfoot, the required ship's maintenance plummeted. With the drop in crew, whole mess kitchens had been abandoned.

Two messes and one galley remained open. The Officers Mess still had the Naval officers, but it also fed the Special Ops personnel. The Chiefs Mess now served all of the remaining Petty Officers and specialists like the engine crew.

Now, part way into the pre-dawn dinner service, the space was packed solid. The long tables were lined with work uniforms and the more casual, off-shift clothing.

Something else had happened while she'd been hovering above the Libyan desert.

Christmas had arrived; damn Barstowe for being right. It was only early December and yet the mess had been transformed.

The overhead pipes had been wound with white and red crepe paper like giant, twisting candy canes. Christmas tree cutouts had been taped to all of the walls. When the MEU was aboard, little of that had happened—the military always being so careful not to offend. When they'd dropped from twenty-five hundred aboard to a few hundred, a vote had been taken. The ship's captain, Lieutenant Commander Boyd Ramis, had allowed a unanimous vote to carry. Holiday décor of any breed or shade was welcome as long as it didn't disrespect others.

There was even a Menorah Section. The Jewish high holiday of Hanukkah was only days away and there was no way she was going to be caught sitting at the foot of a six-foot tall menorah taped to the wall. But she didn't like sitting in front of a Christmas tree either, even if it was just colored paper taped to the bulkhead. It would be like giving in to Barstowe.

Who she couldn't spot anywhere.

Nika had lost a little time enroute and arrived closer to twenty minutes after leaving the hovercraft and Mr. Too-damn-sure-of-himself Ranger, but there was still no sign of Barstowe. She was down the meal line with a full tray before she figured out what was going on. Barstowe was an officer and Spec Ops, he'd automatically think they were meeting a deck above here, up in officer country. Did he even know where this mess was?

She considered braving the foreign land, then considered how damn dumb she'd look toting a full tray up ladderways. She certainly wasn't going to toss out perfectly good food, especially not the way Sly's wife Chief Steward Gail Stowell cooked it. Tonight was meatloaf night—the meat laced with roasted vegetables and Italian spices—one of her favorites.

One last look around and she headed over to her usual spot with the rest of the LCAC crew. A giant reindeer face looked down at their table. There was something weird about the nose that she couldn't make sense of until she was closer. Rudolph's red nose was a seven-inch diameter spare for a Hellfire missile nose cone. It stuck almost a foot out of the wall.

"Good thing that isn't any lower down the wall or it would be terribly phallic," Nika commented as she set down her tray beside Jerome's.

He grunted either an agreement or a greeting, didn't matter which. Dave and Tom turned in unison to look up over their shoulders, then faced each other, then back to her. They even groaned in unison.

"How did we not see that?"

"We're sitting under Rudolph's bright red penis nose."

"*You're* the ones who put it there," Jerome said without looking up from his meal.

"We gotta fix that."

"Well, I'm not touching the damn thing," Nika took her first taste of the meatloaf. "Oh god, that's so good." She waved her fork at the reindeer's nose. "And when some Night Stalker mechanic notices *that* missing out of spares, with red paint over the guidance window, just remember: I got no part of this."

# # #

Barstowe burst out laughing. He couldn't help himself. Nika Maier waving her fork at Rudolph's remarkably phallic nose as if she was going to stab it was just too perfect.

He hadn't even bothered to look for her up in the Officers Mess. They didn't teach Rangers to underestimate opportunities. He'd hooked up with Sly and followed the Chief Petty Officer into the Chiefs Mess, knowing it was shared by all of the enlisted ranks. And it had worked; there she sat threatening poor Rudolph.

Nika looked up at him in alarm as he set down his tray across from her. The spot beside her was also open, but he wanted to look at her so he left that spot for Sly.

He'd wanted to talk with her alone, which was also surprising, but he'd take what he could get away with for now.

"You got the dirt off your face, sir, but there's still some crap in your hair."

Not thinking first, he reached up a hand and ended up grabbing his Santa hat.

Nika's happy smile acknowledged the first point went to her.

"At least she called me 'sir,'" he spoke to Sly. "Some hope there."

"You're Army," Nika didn't give her commander a chance to respond. "I figured you needed to have something go right in your life."

"And my life is so pitiful that calling me 'sir' is a vast improvement?"

"He wasn't listening, was he, Chief?" Nika asked Sly. "Doesn't he get that he's in the Army, not the Navy?"

"Sad, isn't it, Petty Officer Maier?" Sly agreed and ignored Clint's scowl.

Clint opened his mouth to respond, but Dave and Tom had picked up the riff.

"Bunch of ground pounders wouldn't get anywhere if we didn't take them."

"Watch it. Next he'll tell us he doesn't need us because he can always parachute in…as if that was a decent way to travel. Do we tell him that's courtesy of the Air Farce?"

"Don't need either of you," Clint finally managed to get in edgewise.

"How do you figure that, *sir?*" Nika's eyes were sparkling with a laugh.

Clint tapped his Santa-hat covered temple then hooked a thumb over his shoulder at Rudolph's phallic nose cone, "I've got inside connections to alternate transport. Rangers lead the way, Petty Officer Maier. Don't you ever forget that."

Jerome pinged his knife against his water glass like he was ringing a bell, then tipped his head to Clint.

"Second point is apparently mine, Maier. Puts us at tied by my figuring. Your serve."

# # #

Nika tried to remember the last time she'd enjoyed a meal so much. None came readily to mind as she dropped down the ladderways to the LCAC. She was technically off shift for the day, but she always felt better if she checked in on their craft before heading to her bunk. There was a peace and quiet to the empty Well Deck that she'd come to appreciate.

Yet another advantage to the *Peleliu*—she had a vast quiet about her. She'd grown up in noise because Lower Manhattan was never silent. The *George H. W. Bush* and the *Firebolt* had been so crowded that there was never any privacy aboard either vessel.

The bowels of the three-quarters empty *Peleliu* had become her haven. She lay back on the steel ramp at the head of the Well Deck, crossed her boots, and stared up at the ceiling.

The peace wrapped around her. The *Peleliu's* engines, which lay directly beneath her were barely ticking over. They were headed nowhere in particular. Or they were station-holding while command assessed the success of the last mission and planned the next. Whatever was happening was way above her pay grade and she was fine with that.

Lazy Mediterranean waves sloshed against the hull, lulling her.

Let somebody else worry about all that. She was good at what she did and was just fine with doing it. Though she'd like being an LCAC Craftmaster. That would...

She felt the thrum of footsteps where the back of her head rested on the steel deck long before she heard them. Long, measured strides. Moving with utter surety. No man who walked like that could have a single inner doubt. He knew where he stood in the universe—right at its center, by god.

Nika tipped her head back and looked up the ramp as a white pom-pom came into view, followed by a red hat, a white-fur ruff, and an inverted view of a grinning Army Ranger.

"Figured this is where you went to ground," Clint spoke first. "Kind of predictable, Maier."

"Sea floor is a thousand or so meters down, sir. If I go to ground, I'm going to have trouble breathing."

Uninvited, he settled down beside her, then glanced up at the ceiling, almost losing his hat.

It was awfully tempting to tug on the tail of it and just steal the thing. Maybe toss it overboard…except the stern gate was closed and she wasn't sure if she had the energy to climb to an upper deck for so minor a good deed.

"What do see when you look up?"

A man too damn good looking for his own good, she almost answered before she caught herself. "I see stars, galaxies, the wonders of the universe."

His smile was a little sad. "By anyone's scorekeeping, we came out about even at dinner. How about a straight answer for a change?"

"Against my religion, Lieutenant." Besides, by her figuring, he'd come out way ahead just by tracking her down to the Chiefs Mess and sitting with their crew. Brave man, even if he and Sly were close. Brave in more ways than one. She could still see him standing at the calm center as the terrorist camp was subdued around him.

"Jewish," Clint grumbled.

"Not very. New York, though. You can get thrown out of the city for giving a straight answer. Or maybe that *is* the Jewish part of me," she sighed and looked at the ceiling once more. She didn't really know anymore.

After a long couple minutes' silence, Barstowe clambered to his feet.

"Wait," she'd pissed him off, again. He didn't deserve that. "Please."

"Well, for the please, I'll wait." He even attempted humor when he was angry. Yeah, *that* was a path her own family had never thought of. They went for the stoic silence that would echo through the apartment until it was louder than the Manhattan streets right outside their window. Her very first memory was the smothering quality of that blanket of silence that would descend over Dr. and Mrs. Maier.

Nika stood up and joined Clint at the head of the ramp.

Arms crossed, he looked imposing, despite the silly hat. Six feet tall and built solid enough to carry a fifty-pound pack for miles without noticing it. Earned lieutenant the hard way she'd heard, starting enlisted. He showed an awful lot to be impressed by.

"I," she dug for the words, unsure what they were. "I wanted to thank you for what you did tonight."

"My job," his grimaced, his voice gruff with anger.

"No!" She rested a hand on his arm to keep him anchored there and was a little surprised when it worked. "You did more than that. I saw. You…led. You…helped." Each word had to be wrenched from her gut.

There had been no one to help Keila, not even Nika because their schools had been hundreds of miles apart. On hearing the news, she still hadn't rushed to her friend's aid as she should have. Now she'd never know if it would have helped. Learning to live with that had been a total bitch.

Clint had stopped trying to leave and simply watched her passively.

"It's the past that—" she bit that off hard before anything else spilled out.

Still he waited.

"It's important," Nika tried again. "What you did. It's… important," she didn't know what else to say. The only suitable atonement she'd found to offer was herself to the Navy—in Keila's stead.

Clint's face shifted abruptly. Brief shock, then near molten rage. It took him an instant to control his expression.

She looked down, because she couldn't face the compassion that finally showed there.

"Oh, girl," Clint whispered softly and simply wrapped his big arms around her.

Nika let herself be pulled straight in until her nose and forehead rested on his breastbone. She didn't cry. She wasn't going to cry. She didn't believe in tears because they never fixed anything.

"Was it you?" he whispered. And some part of her knew that he wouldn't pull away if it had been.

She could only shake her head. She'd had a couple of scary wrestling matches over the years, but she'd always escaped unscathed. More than some of the aggressors could claim.

He held her there, just held her on that awful precipice as the waves of fury and loss stormed within her, both seeking to suck out her soul. She hung there in silence, safe against a stranger's chest, unable to respond until the storm had subsided enough for her to once again draw breath.

When she did, she smelled soap, clean uniform, and strong man. He smelled solid the way the New York Public Library or the Museum of Natural History did. Rich, deep, solid. Dependable.

"God I'm a mess." How many other stupid things could she think up while having her nose crushed against a man's chest?

"I'd say that you're a very pretty one, but I'm guessing that would piss you off again. Though sure as the day is long, I don't know why."

"It's December, the days are short," she told his chest. "But I do owe you an apology for lashing out. Old parental tapes that I thought I'd long since erased. Always telling me how I *got by* because I was pretty and so why didn't I *use it* to go marry a doctor the way Mom had. And…" Nika sputtered into silence as soon as she realized that she was whining *and* unloading on a man who probably didn't want to be hearing about all of her crap.

"You gonna be okay there, skipper?"

"God no!"

He laughed and stepped her back with his hands on her shoulders until he could look down at her.

"I can see the question, Lieutenant Barstowe," Nika wanted to close her eyes, to hide from the care that shown so clearly beneath the concern. He clearly thought she was losing it and Nika didn't like him thinking that. "When I'm busting ass, I don't have to think, I can just do. Has served me pretty well these last couple tours. But sometimes the past…" She shrugged having no better answer.

"I've always been more of a present tense kind of guy," his tone was light. Not dismissive, but trying to make her feel better. It didn't.

"Clearly not Jewish. We've got five thousand years of paranoia to live up to. And that's without our mothers."

"But as my Pappy says, that ain't no way to be living."

"Please tell me you do *not* call your dad Pappy," she thought that was a movie stereotype.

"Not actually. More like Asshole."

He smiled weakly at the laugh he'd surprised out of her.

"Piece of trash who dodged out when I was six. Left Mama, me, and my little sister holding the bag. But it sounds better when I give my advice in my Pappy's name."

"So you're giving your wisdom to the man who abandoned you? That makes about as much sense as me blaming you for things my mother says."

Clint grimaced. "Hadn't really looked at it that way. He was a useless sack of shit, if the truth be told."

"Useless?" Nika looked hard into Clint's face. "Been making up for that a long time, have you, Lieutenant? Thought you were a present tense kind of guy."

"He's not why I joined."

"Spill it."

"Trade."

"Not a chance in hell!" Nika froze, wrapping her arms tightly about herself and wondered if she was fast enough to dodge around a US Ranger and get up the ramps and ladderways before he could follow.

Anticipating her, he reached out and brushed a comforting hand down her arm. It rooted her to the steel decking; she couldn't run after the kindness of that gesture. He opened his mouth, but she cut him off.

"Don't you apologize because I'm a bitch caught in her own trap," it came out as a snarl he didn't deserve, but she couldn't do anything about that.

He nodded once and again, his hat's pom-pom bouncing as he did so.

"I—" there had to be something she could give him. "I joined because the past gave me no choice. I stay because I have no other answers." It was the most she could give him and it cost her.

He nodded as if he actually understood just how much; his pom-pom again flopping about. Without further requirement, he started speaking. "I joined because of my football coach. Best man I ever met. Mr. Daniels was a Vietnam Vet. A Ranger."

"Bet you went All-State," Nika was surprised she found the tease anywhere inside herself.

His shrug was eloquent.

"Scouted by the colleges."

Again the shrug.

"And the pros?"

He didn't argue. How damn good was he?

"Then what the hell are you doing here, soldier?" She waved her hand taking in the darkened Well Deck, the beached hovercraft, and the fact that they were parked off the Libyan coast.

"Being all I can be." He cut her off before she could give voice to the scoff inside her. "Football is a game. Mr. Dee taught me that what was real was more important; said I was good enough to understand the difference. I introduced him to Mama and we all talked about it. The discipline and structure fit me better than mustard fits a hot dog. Helping, really helping, that's what it's all about." He was nodding with the strength of his own conviction.

"You're a determined sort, aren't you?" Nika felt embarrassed to even be standing beside such a man. Her reasons were lame and elusive by comparison.

"Maybe. Stubborn runs deep in our family; Mama is a very determined sort of lady. She started as an RN and now runs a major hospital back home in Little Rock, so it's in my blood too. 'Course there was a drawback to introducing them."

"What was that?" But she had a guess. At her smile, Clint merely nodded. His football coach had done more with Clint's mom than talk about her son.

She wasn't feeling all mushy about Clint Barstowe because he'd held her. It wasn't because he such a sweet man who worshipped his Mama. What she did next was because he was just such a good man.

She reached up…and yanked off his Santa hat.

"Hey!" Clint made a grab for it and she switched it between hands behind her back.

"Not a chance am I kissing a man wearing a Santa hat."

"What have you got against Sant—"

Clint froze. She could see the look in his eyes shift, inspecting her face to make sure she meant what she'd said.

Nika did her best to not give away any hints on what he should do next.

A moment later Nika knew there was one quality of a US Army Ranger that she'd never doubt again. Rangers were men of action.

# # #

The cold shower hadn't done shit for shutting down his thoughts about Nika Maier, especially not with her standing inches away and doing her best to look so innocent with his Santa hat held behind her back.

Sparring with her over dinner had only added to the heat. But that heat had shifted as he held her down here in the heart of the *Peleliu*. Held her while she'd proved to both herself and to him just how strong she really was.

The heat didn't go away, not by a long shot. And not a chance was he turning down an offer to kiss her, but it didn't happen the way his libido had imagined.

Clint had thought a tussle with Nika would be fun. Maybe somehow they could ignore weightier matters and just heat up each other's blood with a bit of play. What he didn't figure on was how her cheeks would feel cradled between his palms, or how those big, dark eyes watched him as he leaned down to brush their lips together.

Her hands didn't come up to hold or touch him, but he could feel her rising on her toes, adding pressure as the kiss deepened. The playfulness that he'd anticipated, fantasized about—her innate merriness—was instead a steady truth.

Clint was not just kissing some woman.

He was kissing Nika Maier.

She was a hundred percent present right now as they pressed together. Not their bodies. His hands did not move from her face to once again hold the lithe strength of her fine form, because even when she'd been leaning against him in misery there were some things a man couldn't help but notice. Only their lips met. And Clint knew he'd never received such a kiss in his life. Like an honest gift.

He'd been correct before the mission.

Nika Maier was a serious kind of woman and kissing her was a serious kind of business. They hadn't even begun and he was already in over his head.

Of course if this was drowning, someone please sign him up.

"That," she whispered against his lips when they finished, "can never happen again."

"Are you mad?" He couldn't believe his ears. "Girl, that has so got to happen again."

"Nope. Allow me to prove it," and she tugged the Santa hat back on his head. "See? I'll never kiss a man wearing a Santa hat."

It took all of his self control to not drag her against him and prove her wrong. Or lay her down on the steel ramp and finish the job for both of them.

But Nika Maier was a serious kind of woman he had to remind himself.

There'd be another time. A woman didn't smile at you the way she was smiling if there wasn't.

Best move?

Back away slowly, like from a mine about to explode.

For now.

"You *will* kiss the man in the hat one day," he found some tease in his suddenly dry throat.

"Sorry to crush your hopes, Lieutenant Santa, but it's not going to happen."

"That against your religion too?"

"Nope. You just look too silly for words while wearing it. Never is your answer."

"Oh, I gots me some patience, girl. I swear on a pack o' blue-tick hounds that I does," he let his Arkansas through as if he was some country hick and not from the largest city in the state.

"Nobody as patient as this Navy gal."

"So, you kissed me just to make sure I wouldn't sleep a wink today?"

"You're the one who kissed me, soldier. And of course that's the only reason I *let* you do it."

"Problem is, sailor," he brushed a finger down that ever so soft skin of her cheek and her eyelids fluttered half closed. He'd swear she sighed though he'd wager his next month's pay that she'd never admit it. "It backfired and you won't be sleeping a wink either."

"Bet you twenty I will."

"Done!" He raised his palm and she high-fived it to seal the deal.

Chapter 5

*C*rap!

Nika stared at the ceiling of her berth. Normally she'd be in a four-berth with three other petty officers. But because of the light crew needed to operate the *Peleliu,* she'd been able to scrounge a berth of her own. It wasn't luxurious, she could touch either side wall at the same time and she didn't need to reach a full stretch twice to span the other direction, but it was hers alone. There were other female petty officers—the Navy was twenty percent female after all—but she had little to do with them since switching from the Flight Deck to the LCAC.

Double crap!

She was going to owe Lieutenant too-damn-sure-of-himself Barstowe twenty bucks if she didn't get to sleep in the next fifteen minutes. How was she supposed to know that the arrogant prick would be such a damn good kisser?

Of course if that had been the only issue, she could have slept fine. After all, a kiss that paralyzes you from the neck down happened…approximately…never. Yet Clint's had. It had been so perfect, so intense, that she hadn't even thought to raise a hand to touch his face. To see how his shoulder fit the curve of her palm. To hang on for dear life as her knees melted.

Still, that shouldn't have been a problem.

Nor the verbal teasing, which had been nothing more than good fun.

No, it was the way he'd held her before that was such an issue. No one held Nika Maier when she was miserable. Not former lovers, not friends, and surely not her parents.

Yet Clint had done exactly that. He'd held her and just let her be herself. He hadn't petted and patted and told her not to cry. He'd simply held her and offered comfort and, just maybe, some understanding.

The alarm jolted her like an electric shock and she slapped at it.

Coffee.

A shower, then coffee.

That was going to be the only cure for Clint Barstowe. Total avoidance. Maybe she'd be lucky and not see him today.

Chapter 6

Clint had kept his boys on the run all night. They'd started with a tactical debrief of last night's mission—studying every move to see how it could have been improved. Then they'd fully serviced every piece of equipment they'd taken into the field. After that, he'd gotten them up on the deck for target practice.

The *Peleliu* was eight hundred feet long, an easy distance for a Ranger, but only if they kept in constant practice.

The Night Stalkers had their helos off the deck running their own exercise—precision shooting at small marker floats during low-level, high-speed passes. Clint set up a shooting range on the blacked out deck to rack up some night-scope practice. There was just enough roll on the ship that his Rangers had to compensate for the nine-tenths of second of travel required by the special-issue subsonic rounds he'd selected—the targets had time to shift several inches in the time it took the bullet to travel the length of the deck.

With the suppressors, their practice was almost completely silent—no sharp crack of standard-issue rounds moving at twice the speed of sound. Just a soft pop and the click of the bolt auto-loading the next round in the chamber. Even the bright ping of ejected rounds sang in the quiet night.

While the helos were off deck, he ran his men through a few hundred rounds apiece. Two of the guys were solidly ready for the next level course during their next rotation stateside. They were turning into top snipers; he could see it in their motions as well as their consistent results.

Now, after a long, sweaty night—and another ice cold shower that hadn't helped anything—he'd wandered forward to the gaming room.

There was a projection TV aimed at a white-painted section of the hull with a cluster of occupied steel chairs circled around it. Some ball game. Never held his interest—that was his past, not his present—but the guys and some of the Navy gals were into it. They screened movies here too, and the posters that had been shipped out papered the walls in a blinding array of color and tech; not a whole lot of romantic comedies for this crowd.

Board games, cards (that were forbidden to be used for gambling according to the lone white sign among the sea movies posters, so they of course were used for nothing else), and some table games.

He'd checked on his men, about a third of them were here. Lamar and Ruiz were in one of their intense speed chess tournaments—ten seconds maximum per move. It made him twitchy just to watch them. They could rack up dozens of games a night and he couldn't beat either of them no matter how much time they gave him.

Hanson was sitting nearby, glaring at another chess board. No one sat opposite him. Hanson didn't like opponents: *Always messing up my games, Lieutenant.* He only played against himself no matter how often he was razed about playing *with* himself. Clint had watched his slow, thoughtful games a time or two and decided that Hanson was out of his league as well.

Clint had always been more of an action man. Pool, which was impossible to play on a rolling ship, had paid for more than a few of his drinking nights back in his early days. Of the table games available aboard ship, he rocked the foosball table and soon gravitated to the back of the crowd gathering there to watch a Ranger versus Navy matchup.

"Damn it! I knew my luck was too good to last."

Clint looked down to see the top of Nika's head close beside him. He hadn't even noticed her approach.

"I guess I need a different kind of luck," Nika continued. "Can't see squat either. Just Rangers getting beat by Navy anyway, so it's nothing new."

"Well," he went for Southern friendly. "If you weren't so short, might have better a better view. Could always sit on my shoulders, Petty Officer. Must say though, I surely do not know why the Navy grows them so short."

"No chance in hell, Lieutenant Barstowe," she cricked her neck back to glance up at him from so close and looked as if she was going to snicker at his hat's white pom-pom.

Then it chose that moment to slide forward and dangle in his eye and her snicker turned into a smirk.

"I'd thought it was going to be a good morning," her shrug was one of eloquent resignation. "Guess not."

"What's wrong with this morning?" He brushed aside the pom-pom that went to dangle in front of his other eye.

Her smile only grew. Well, he know how to take care of that.

"Owe me money from our bet, do you?"

"Go to hell, sir," her looked of too damned pleased with herself went away quickly enough.

"Probably will, sailor. I probably will. But I'll be twenty dollars richer when I do. A passel better than a poke in the eye." And even now he could hear Hell beckoning with the thoughts he was thinking. Thoughts he shouldn't be thinking at all, especially not in the midst of a crowd. But if she lost a night's sleep over their brief kiss, then at least they were on equal footing there.

Then her eyes narrowed and he wondered if he should cut for the exit while he still had a chance.

"Air hockey, Lieutenant?"

"Yes, Petty Officer Maier. That is what the table behind you is called."

"Do you *play* air hockey, Lieutenant?"

"Been known to whip some Navy ass from time to time."

Without another word, she turned and walked toward the table. He instantly regretted the "Navy ass" remark as his attention was riveting on Nika's fine one. She wasn't a "hippy" woman, but she displayed a form just designed for a man's hand to cradle. To cradle while pulling her in tight and kissing her like—

"You chickening out on me?" Nika called back without even turning.

Somehow she knew he wasn't following. He just hoped she didn't know where his thoughts had wandered off to. Clint got his feet in motion and used his longer legs to catch up without hurrying.

At the air hockey table he was chagrined to see that Jerome, the LCAC's mechanic and assistant Loadmaster, was kicking Sergeant Dupree's butt. The eight-foot table, full regulation size, looked like a pool table without the pockets. It hissed softly with the air it was pumping out of the myriad holes in its smooth plastic surface.

The red three-and-a-quarter inch puck skittered frictionlessly across the surface at lightning speeds. Jerome and Dupree each wielded small plastic mallets with rounded handles on top, trying to protect the narrow slot of a goal in the center of either end.

Each mallet's sharp crack against the puck sent it ricocheting off the left and right sides of the table's edge, then zipping toward the opponent's goal. Desperate attempts to block it with the tiny mallet were made and, impossibly, succeeded fairly often.

Except that it succeeded far less often for Dupree than for Jerome.

In under three minutes, Jerome was the victor at a score of seven to three. Clint offered Dupree a sympathetic look, but it wasn't a good one, a Ranger should be able to whip a swabbie at anything.

Jerome took out Tom and then Dave from the LCAC's crew: seven-zip, seven-two.

Clint felt a little more sympathetic toward Dupree after that; Jerome was clearly very good. He spotted Sly in the gathering crowd.

"What about you, Chief?"

"Don't like to shame my crew, Lieutenant."

That earned him the expected round of razzing, especially after Jerome beat him seven-one.

Clint was only too happy to add his own round of abuse onto Sly's head.

"Let's see you take him, *Lieutenant.*" Nika drawled out Clint's rank like an insult.

He'd rather play foosball, but figured that was no longer an option. He liked the energy of foosball games. They tended to be rowdier because they moved a little slower and they were played two-on-two instead of one-on-one like air hockey. He could hear a roar from the crowd over there, half cheers and half groans as someone nailed a winning goal with a sharp rattle of the small plastic ball rocketing into the pocket.

Air hockey was silent, fast, and very intense, much like the woman standing beside him.

Knowing his Ranger reputation was on the line, no way would he be backing down in front of Nika Maier.

He moved to the table and went up on his toes. Been a while since he'd played air hockey.

# # #

Just as she'd expected. Jerome nailed the first two goals against Clint almost immediately.

But then Clint got one back.

Nika started watching less of the game and more of the man. Despite his size, Clint moved lightly. And those big hands that had occupied so much of her waking thoughts last night had a control and finesse that was unexpected. Just as how gentle they had been when he'd cradled her face to kiss her. It had shocked her into stillness not to be grabbed or pinned or dragged forward, but instead to be cradled. For a top-tier warrior to possess such a soft caress had been an electrifying contrast—right down to her toes.

She liked Clint. And even before that kiss, had been thinking what fun it might be to bed the man. Big, handsome warriors didn't typically do much for her, but Clint didn't fit any of the stereotypes that usually went along with those two attributes.

A Ranger Lieutenant who could laugh at himself. Who could wear a Santa hat just to make people smile. And who could kiss like…

A sharp crack and the puck hummed as it flew past her ear before she could even flinch aside. It wasn't like Jerome to send one airborne.

She focused back on the game and was shocked when Clint sunk a goal within seconds of returning the puck to play and announced the score, "Six-four."

Nobody beat Jerome.

Well, almost nobody.

Her crewmate held on for seven-five, but he went down.

Clint looked over at her, "Air hockey, Maier. Do *you* play air hockey, Petty Officer?"

"Might," Nika answered and ignored the roll of soft laughter from her team.

"Any good? Or should I go get a Ranger so that I can have a decent challenge?"

"Care to put a twenty on that, Lieutenant?" Nika asked him with all of the innocence she could muster.

"No gambling is allowed aboard ship, Petty Officer." She have liked winning back the money that she'd lost betting she'd be able to sleep last night.

"I—" then she glanced aside at her teammates. She wasn't about to explain that particular lapse in front of her teammates. "We'll make it a friendly game then." But she'd make sure that there was hell to pay later.

Being magnanimous, he gave her first control of the puck... which she sunk in the first three seconds of play.

"One-zero," she offered in her mildest tone. There was a small buzz of laughter by the few people paying any attention to the game.

Clint smile went from easy to cautious. By the time they were at three-zero, even that was gone.

Flying an air hockey table was like flying a hovercraft, it was in her blood. She didn't focus on the table. Instead she let her vision blur slightly and allowed her body to react without trying to think about plans or strategies.

A puck rocketed off the mid-point of the left bank and she'd shift her weight right to flick her wrist left for the block. A drive down the center could be deflected into her own corner so that she could take control.

Clint got control of the puck and called a time-out.

"Ten seconds," someone called out. Jerome. Stepping in as referee. They didn't normally use one in these games.

Nika didn't move, didn't shift.

She was in the zone and Clint needing a break wasn't going to ruin her focus. She waited out the break, counting beats of her heart.

"Back in play," Jerome announced.

Clint fired a lightning shot and even though she was ready, there was the sickening thunk of the puck sliding home.

"Three-one," Jerome declared. That turned a few people's heads; typically Jerome was the only one able to score against her at all.

By four-three, Nika could no longer merely dominate the table as she typically did. And she began getting a feel for Clint's style of play. It was as unexpected as his kiss.

The powerful warrior played with lightness and agility.

At five-five, she identified something else. He played with…a sense of fun. Little wrist flicks would tease her about how the puck might fly one way and then he'd send it the other. She ignored the growing crowd.

She became aware of more than the table, which was sufficient to beat most players. Nika started noticing the player himself. The way his shoulders would shift the instant before a hard drive ahead. The furrowing of his brow on a hard block.

After six-five they had a roaring battle that must have lasted at least a minute. A typical time to goal was under twenty seconds in air hockey, but he kept anticipating her moves with such grace.

# # #

"Six-six. Game point," Jerome's declaration was music to Clint's ears and he resisted swiping at the sweat on his brow.

They'd gathered a packed crowd now. Even the foosball table had fallen to silence—the ball game was still on the TV, but no one was watching it—everyone straining to see over each other's shoulders. Apparently no one kept up with Nika and now he knew why.

She was the best player he'd ever faced. She played with a blinding focus, so intense that he could feel it washing across the table. Her gaze never wavered; her stance never altered. No time out called.

Game point.

She brought the puck into play with an unexpectedly soft move. It ricocheted back to her barely moving by air hockey standards. Far to the side, it hadn't even been an attack on the goal.

Twice more she'd let it practically drift down the table, drawing his attention well clear of the goal.

The next shot came so viciously hard that it was all he could do to block it.

Each rebound she fired back with the speed of an M134 Gatling gun.

He finally managed to break the attack and gain control of the puck, only barely missing sinking it in his own goal in the process. He fired some testing shots down the table, mixed with tapping it side to side in his own end so that he could gauge her reactions.

And somehow he knew, he just knew he had her.

He built up to it slowly.

A double-corner to the right, a straight in to the left and again to the right.

And then she shifted left in anticipation—just as he'd set her up to do—and he fired a hard bank to the right for all he was worth.

The entire hall was silent. Rangers and Navy alike were standing up on benches and tables to see the game so that the two of them were at the center of a rising bowl of humanity.

The puck flew toward her goal and—

Nika didn't block it.

She didn't *just* block it.

Moving in some impossible state of speed and precision, she hammered all of the power of his strike into a straight drive directly toward the center of his goal.

There was no way to move fast enough; it just wasn't physically possible.

The puck slammed into Clint's goal slot with the sharp *Snap!* that only occurred at the highest speeds.

There was a moment of perfect silence in which the only sound was the clattering of the puck as it tumbled to a rest inside his goal.

"Seven-six! Game!" Jerome shouted above the roar that erupted in the next instant. "The champ retains her title!"

Clint raised his mallet to his forehead and saluted her with it.

Ignoring the congratulations of her crew and others, she saluted him back the same way. And didn't turn those big brown eyes away from his for a hypnotically long moment.

Clint really needed to get this woman somewhere alone and he needed to do it now.

But Nika turned away from him as if the air between them wasn't glowing with the heat. He tracked her as far as he could. Only at the far door did she turn back to look at him.

The heat was still there. She displayed no signs of triumph, no feral smile of victory upon her features. Nika Maier simply stood and looked at him across the room and the dispersing crowd.

Kept looking until he realized that she was departing by the hatch that was closest to her bunk. She waited until some form of recognition must have passed over his features, then she turned and walked away.

The fact that he didn't want a woman that intense was no longer a choice; he did. In the process of exfiltrating himself from the room without being too obvious, he got sucked into a game of foosball with Mitchum against Dave and Tom from the LCAC crew. He lost miserably and quickly much to Mitchum's dismay.

He then exited through the opposite hatchway closest to his own quarters. Rangers didn't sneak up on targets. Well, they did, but it was for purposes of stealth and surprise not for hiding something from your own crew. But this time he wanted no one to know where he was headed.

As he doubled back through the silent corridors of the vast ship, climbed ladderways and ducked through hatches, he began to wonder quite what he was doing. Clandestine meetings weren't his style.

And with a shock at the very moment he arrived silently outside Nika Maier's bunk, Clint realized that Nika wasn't his style either. His, ah, encounters were invariably with long, leggy women who knew the meaning of the word fling.

Despite his doubts, his hand raised to knock on her door, but it was cracked open.

What are you doing, Clint? You don't want this.

No. But he wanted her.

He eased the door open, stepped in, and closed it behind him.

Chapter 7

N*ika hadn't heard Clint* arrive outside her door, even as he blocked the corridor light that shone through the crack. Again that unexpected lightness of a Special Operations soldier.

She had no doubt that he would come, even if she did wonder at the invitation she'd offered. In the eight years of four tours and a blur of deployments, she'd been with a Marine pilot for six months and a Petty Officer from the engine crew for three. Other than a couple brief encounters while on leave, that had been the extent of her relationships since that day she walked off the college campus and into the military.

She never went into sex thinking it was just casual, even if she quickly concluded that's all it could ever be with that person. But with Clint, she'd decided that casual was the only safe way to go other than none at all. None at all didn't sound like fun and she'd pretty much signed off on discarding that option.

This doesn't mean anything she'd kept assuring herself while she waited. That would be the answer. *This is only about assuaging the heat that had inexplicably built between them.* But how had it become so charged in just these last few days?

It was only when Clint knelt in front of the lone desk chair she'd sat in, that she focused on him.

Of its own volition, her hand reached out to stroke his cheek; her slender fingers so light against his darker complexion. His day's growth of beard gave texture to his smooth skin. She ran her thumb back and forth over the grain of it not quite daring to focus on those dark eyes that were studying her so intently.

But neither could she speak.

Instead, she gently brushed his hat off his head and leaned forward until their lips met. Neither of them made a sound. No groans, moans, or sighs— there was simply connection.

When his hand rested on her knee and slid up and down her thigh, it was as natural as the arm she slid around his neck to hang on. The transition from sitting in her chair to straddling his lap happened as smoothly as the hovercraft coming to rest in the Well Deck where it belonged.

They explored together.

His hands shifted to cradle her behind and hold her close to him with such easy strength. She allowed herself to tip back so that his lips could explore her neck and where her collarbone met the line of her Navy blue t-shirt.

"I—"

She pulled herself back in to stop his words with her mouth. This wasn't about words. When she did, he'd clearly gotten the message.

It was a bit of a struggle because he kept holding her so close, but she worked his t-shirt free and pulled it off over his head.

His arms were the size of her thighs and rippled with muscle every time he moved. His chest was a thing of glory and she yanked off her own t-shirt and bra so that she could revel in the feel of skin against skin.

He kept one of those big arms around her waist and rose to his feet as if she didn't weigh anything.

Once they gained their feet, it didn't take long to shed the rest of their clothes.

She stepped back a single step, all that her berth allowed, to admire the man before her.

"You're beautiful, Lieutenant Barstowe."

"I think that's my line, Petty Officer Maier."

"What, *You're beautiful, Lieutenant Barstowe?* The mirror is behind you if you're that much of a narcissist."

He didn't glance over his shoulder, but she did. And the view had a great deal to recommend it.

She felt suddenly awkward and shy. Nika had never been one to stand naked to be admired. She was far more likely to slip out of her clothes under the covers with the lights off. But Clint was a man well worth looking at, and not just the impressive proof of his attraction to her.

He was battered, his skin was far from perfect, as you'd expect from an Army Ranger with a decade of service. But it gave him more character. He'd seen things, done things, and traveled through them to end up magnificent.

"If one of us doesn't do something soon," he dragged his gaze back up from her body to look her in the eyes, "I'm going to die standing here and that will—"

She shoved hard against the center of his chest.

# # #

Clint tried to stumble back, but there was nowhere to go. Maier's bunk caught him behind the knees and he landed flat on his back with a squeal of springs.

She produced a foil packet of protection and slid it over him. Her fingers brushing down him almost undid his control. Then, without hesitation or preamble, she straddled over him and took him into her body. As forthright in sex as she was in words.

He looked down at where they were joined, startled by the contrast. Her slim figure and light skin such a contrast to his own, yet they fit as if they'd been custom designed for the match.

He let his hands travel over her torso and her palm-filling breasts that fit her so perfectly. He marveled at the contrast between the soft skin and gentle contact when compared with the mind-blowing power of his connection so deep inside her.

When he cupped both her breasts, she clamped her hands over his, pinning them in place and interlacing their fingers so that they seemed to blur together, light and dark, slim and powerful. It was as if their hands formed some kind of artwork that he'd never understand but couldn't stop admiring.

She leaned her weight against his palms as she tipped her head back and exposed a neck that would put a swan to shame.

Clint knew he had never been with such an amazing woman.

And when the release slammed into her and then him moments later, he also knew he'd never been with a woman he wanted so badly to have again right away. A plan of action that would be only a little delayed.

Chapter 8

Sly shook her shoulder as Nika almost planted her nose in her third cup of coffee. The caffeine was not coursing through her system and turning her into Wonder Woman… nor Supergirl…not even Batgirl. Navy coffee was supposed to be able to cure all ills, but it sure wasn't working this morning.

"Mission briefing, Maier. Let's go."

She blinked at Chief Stowell stupidly, stupidly like when she'd been a fresh recruit in way over her head. She stared down at her breakfast, barely half finished. She'd gone a dozen nights with very little sleep, but could find few reasons to complain. As a matter of fact, her main complaint at the moment was that the caffeine that had sustained her through two weeks of having Clint as a lover no longer seemed to have any effect.

She really needed to get some sleep, but men like Clint Barstowe only happened in the movies or novels, not real life. So, she greedily took all he could give and, being a US Ranger, he never stopped delivering. It didn't matter if they'd had a brutal exercise or another mission ashore, each night he found his way to her bed.

"Tonight we must sleep," she'd complain.

"Uh-huh," Barstowe would agree, join her in the narrow bunk, and in a heartbeat the resolve was gone and soon the night as well. Sometimes they talked, but never anything deep or that lasted long. Childhood, school, service, missions.

It was so unreal that she could almost pretend that none of it had really happened. Maybe everything since the air hockey game had just been some sort of a lack-of-sleep-induced hallucination.

She'd believed that right after the air hockey match. She had figured that they'd sate their initial blast of lust and be done. Nika never kept lovers for long. Her early relationships were often measured in hours. Not that the guys didn't want to come back. But if Nika knew there was no future with them—which was often painfully obvious—she saw no point in a rematch.

Instead—unless it really was just a massive hallucination—the last two weeks had only been the beginning with Clint. That first night, without a word spoken, Clint had swept her away on a fantasy that had lasted until the last hour before the alarm clock. She'd woken alone, which was decent of him. But the next night…and the one following…and the time she'd gotten him alone in the aft lockers…then on a bunk at the back of the empty Marine barracks or…

And the sex wasn't only lock and load. There had been dreamy hours of languid exploration as well, until one or the other of them begged for release.

Sly nudged her again.

Present tense. Caffeine insufficient. She looked up at her commander with bleary eyes.

"I don't do briefings. That's you, Chief."

"Craftmaster needs to be in the briefing. Today that's you, Maier. Snap to."

She didn't understand but she snapped to, tipping back her dry coffee cup in vain hope that some stray drop would instill a positive effect, then dumping her tray at the cleanup station. Just her luck that on a day when she needed an extra eight hours sleep and a whole lot more time than that to do some thinking, she was being dragged into a briefing.

On all of the previous training runs, Sly had taken the briefing, then sat close behind her during the training mission and given her constant feedback and tips. Craftmaster implied that she would be in command on this run.

But Lieutenant Clint Barstowe hadn't given her any time to think; which wasn't entirely his fault even if she wished it was. His need for her had been wholly matched by her own surprising need in turn. The only reason it could have built so high was because it had been so long since she'd taken a man to her bed. Get him there, use him to their mutual enjoyment, and then everything could just go back to normal…except it wasn't.

In under two minutes they were entering Lieutenant Commander Boyd Ramis' office four decks above the mess hall at the Flight Deck level.

She hadn't been in the converted pilots' ready room since the Marines left and Boyd had taken over the space. Instead of a dozen Marine pilots lounging around in full flight gear waiting for a mission go, it was now the LCDR's office. At one end, he'd bolted down a big desk, immaculate except for a framed picture of his family. Behind him hung an American flag and a picture of the President looking exactly the same as he did on every other US command—kindly but strong. The prior President had looked just the same. Same photographer or Photoshop? Maybe it was part of the swearing in ceremony. They injected the victor with a drug that made them look kindly and strong, but by the end of four or eight years they became so gray and haggard that their own mother wouldn't recognize them. Who on Earth could possibly want that job? It never ceased to amaze her.

There were couches, several armchairs, and a half dozen simple metal foldouts with padded seats. The room was already crowded when she and Sly arrived. She considered another cup but she guessed that her bladder would not be impressed by the idea later. Besides, her hands were shaking a bit. If her body was feeling the caffeine, why wasn't her brain? Now that was a raw deal.

One long line of windows looked out on the Flight Deck where the crews were unwrapping the helicopters for a flight. When not in the air, they were kept under shrouds because no one wanted to show off that the 5D was flying stealth gear. Out the other window was an amazing view of the Mediterranean Sea. A lighter blue than the Atlantic, which made no sense, but it was true. Unlike an aircraft carrier, the *Peleliu* was alone on the ocean. No other vessel nor any land in sight.

The sun had just kissed the horizon and she could practically hear it sizzle as it was doused from sharp yellow to dull red and sank into the sea. Clear skies and calm seas, good for night operations. Then she looked out the other windows and saw clouds looming up over the African continent that didn't look nearly so pleasant.

But no one was explaining why she was here. She was one of only two here that weren't officers—Chief Petty Officer Sly Stowell, still an enlisted man, was the other. Colonel Michael Gibson of Delta Force. The women of SOAR were here in force: Captains Claudia Jean Gibson and Kara Moretti, Second Lieutenant O'Malley, and Chief Warrant Lola Maloney. The only male from the Night Stalkers was the long, lean Texan Justin Roberts who flew the monstrous Chinook helicopter.

Nika decided that an extra cup of coffee was a good idea after all. Maybe the caffeine had all settled in her lower extremities and she just needed to raise the tide level in her body until it reached her head. She turned toward the urn and bumped her nose on the center of someone's chest. And that's when the last of this day's luck finally ran out the rest of the way.

"Petty Officer Maier," Clint greeted her.

"Lieutenant Barstowe," she tried not to admire the chest at eye level that she had so enjoyed curling up against.

But he would know as well as she did that officers and enlisted didn't mix—even if that was only one of the many things they'd never talked about. They especially didn't mix in public on a ship. And double that when she didn't know what to make of it either.

Yet it was the smell of him, the feel of that gentle bump together, that finally brought her wide awake.

# # #

Clint did his best to look away from her, but it was hard. Nika had revealed herself to him so completely, that it was impossible to not think about her. That first night, she had simply abandoned herself to the fire raging between them. Every attempt he made to bury that fire had only ignited it afresh. There was a life, a deep-rooted vitality that drove Nika Maier. Being permitted to share in that was a gift indeed.

He followed her over to the coffee pot, because she made that look like a very good idea. She made everything look like a very good idea.

That first night he'd slipped from her room with no one the wiser, and spent the hour between then and breakfast pumping iron and taking a shower. One luxury of having the *Peleliu* so under-populated was that there were few restrictions on showers because he'd needed one, and not just from lifting weights. The nights following, he'd slept like a dead man when he could—when she'd let him. Nika was very creative in how she woke a man.

He knew he was just asking for a court-martial; a realization that had caught up with him that first night just as he bench-pressed two-twenty...and almost dropped the bar on himself.

Had it been worth it? In retrospect he'd have to say *Hell, yeah!* He not only had never had a woman like Nika. He'd never even dreamed of it. She'd given and given until he didn't know a man could take so much or want to give so much back. A night like that could carry a man a long damn way. A dozen nights was close to killing him.

Imagining a lifetime of nights like that, well, no way this boy was that lucky. Besides, there had to be a catch somewhere; a "gotcha" like The Bitch and Mr. Used Car.

Had it been worth risking getting Nika in trouble or discharged? Much different answer there, but their attempts to discuss the risks hadn't lasted longer than their first touch firing them upward once more.

Clint reasoned that their relationship across branches of the military wouldn't be a big deal, except they were in a shared chain of command. Sort of. Actually, the chain of command aboard this mash-up of a ship was far less than clear.

He swallowed back his first dose of Navy sludge and felt better for it. Even the Army didn't make coffee this black. At the moment, he needed it as he scanned the room.

Lieutenant Commander, Navy, Boyd Ramis, a thin, almost patrician man, thought he was in charge, and perhaps he was—of everything except where his ship was going and the missions themselves.

Chief Warrant 3, Army, Lola Maloney, a model beautiful woman with flowing mahogany hair, was in charge of the Night Stalkers' missions—which was now the driving force of the ship. The fact that several superior rank officers appeared to report to her only made that side of it murkier. Though there was no question about Maloney being the right woman to be in charge; she was a complete natural as a leader.

And there was Colonel Gibson, Army but Delta, a non-descript man if not for his shining blue eyes, who Clint guessed was actually calling the shots behind the scenes. He also had a very small team who appeared to be permanently embedded with these Night Stalkers just as he was.

Behind all of them there lurked Joint Special Operations Command and no one ever knew what JSOC was doing until they pointed and said go.

What was a mere Lieutenant in charge of a platoon of the Army's 75th Rangers supposed to actually know?

What Clint knew for certain was that if he leaned in just a few inches more as he added two sugars to his own coffee, he and Nika would have been embracing. Her eyes were bright with fatigue, but she smelled of soap and showers—a combination he definitely didn't want to be thinking about because soaping up Petty Officer Maier had been a serious amount of fun. Toweling her down even more so. Her hair, still a little damp in spots, ruffled about her face, and again those big brown eyes had focused on him briefly with complete frankness.

Most other women would have backed up a step, looked away, had some hidden layers that men weren't allowed to see. Nika Maier let him see that the wonders of last night had not existed solely in his imagination, as he'd briefly feared this morning.

That had led him back to his "no way in hell was he getting snarled up with a woman ever again." Hadn't Mama proved that marching solo was definitely a better way to go? His body had other ideas and they were slowly getting through to his brain.

"Lieutenant? *Lieutenant?*" Nika's voice sharpened, cutting through the thoughts that had him leaning in even closer though her voice was little more than a whisper.

"Uh, yeah?"

She tipped her head ever so slightly to the right.

LCDR Ramis had moved to stand behind his desk and was calling the meeting to order.

He heard her laugh in his head, though she only smiled. Then she turned and sat in one of the fold-out metal chairs next to Sly.

Clint fumbled for a moment and ended up taking the last open seat, next to Colonel Gibson. The D-boy was a couple inches shorter than he was, but Gibson still made Clint feel small; he was simply that good.

During each of the terrorist camp raids, he'd done his best to live up to the Colonel's standard.

Gibson thumped him on the shoulder in a surprisingly friendly fashion.

"What?" Clint looked at him in surprise.

He was looking pleased, but still didn't speak.

"What?"

Gibson's smile shifted slightly.

Clint couldn't read it.

"Well done," the Colonel said softly. At first Clint had thought Gibson was congratulating him for what he and Nika were doing while the rest of the ship slept. But then he recalled Gibson would have had a bird's eye view from the helicopter he'd been circling in above the third terrorist camp they'd raided in two weeks.

"Thanks, I lead good men."

Gibson's eyes narrowed for a long moment, then he nodded once more. His enigmatic smile was back as he once more thumped Clint's shoulder in a friendly fashion. Sadness? Pity perhaps? But neither made any sense.

Clint had distinct feeling that he'd completely missed the point and had no idea where to go looking for it.

# # #

She was going to kill both of them, Nika just didn't know in which order.

Lieutenant Clint Barstowe for costing her yet another night's sleep and stirring up all sorts of things she didn't want stirred up? Because her first-ever attempt at having just casual sex had backfired on her like hell. Not letting him speak that first night had been an even worse mistake than allowing it. Clint had used it as an opportunity to morph their sex into lovemaking and the smallest gestures into romantic silliness. Over the last two weeks he'd continued to expand on the theme. And his worst offense? She couldn't seem to get enough of him.

Or should she off Colonel Michael Gibson first for that knowing smile and thumping congratulations to Clint for being the first man to bed Nika Maier in over three years?

Maybe she'd wait until the next time they were lined up together and she had the controls on the LCAC. Two for one with old Number 316. Not a jury of women anywhere would convict her.

Nika glanced at the other women in the room—the power-houses of the Night Stalkers. Lola was saying something about heli-assets and Trisha was teasing her about it. But Claudia was also observing the antics of her husband Michael, apparently unusual enough that it had her brow furrowed. Claudia started scanning the room until her gaze met Nika's, then they widened slightly in surprised recognition—perhaps reading Nika's intent to commit murder, or at least severe retribution. A glance back at the two men before returning. Nika thought she saw the austere Captain soften in…not pity, but perhaps in commiseration.

Then Sly nudged her in the ribs. Great, now he was in on the whole joke and she'd have to run him down as well. If she could manage it without ending up in the brig, at least she'd get a shot at driving the hovercraft in his place. Then—

He nudged her again before nodding toward the other side of the room.

"—and Petty Officer Maier," LCDR Ramis was saying, "will be driving the LCAC for this exercise."

She did her best to hide her gasp of surprise with a simple nod of acknowledgement that didn't fool Sly for a second. Thankfully it turned out to be the beginning, not the end of the briefing. As Ramis laid out the plan, Nika was relieved that Sly was off the hook. Now the only men in need of a lesson in humility were both from the Army and not the Navy. That they were two of the most amazing warriors she'd ever met was a different issue. She'd have to be sneaky.

Thankfully, the Navy had trained her body well enough that it took notes even while her mind continued on to other matters.

Aircraft carrier three hundred kilometers away. Exercises with Rangers and Night Stalkers enroute. Refuel, cargo pickup. Return.

No one was saying what kind of cargo or why it wouldn't be more efficient to just send the Night Stalkers' big Chinook.

Captain Roberts sat back in a chair with his white cowboy hat tipped back on his head, looking as casual as if this was a night on the range around a campfire and not a pre-mission briefing, but she suspected that he didn't miss a thing. He flew for the 5D which put the stamp of excellence on his forehead as clearly as the cowboy hat.

As the briefing broke up, Claudia crossed her path without making it appear out of the ordinary. She'd been with the outfit for over a year but they'd never exchanged a word outside of operations. Nor did they this time. Claudia simply squeezed her shoulder for a long moment, then moved past her and out toward the Flight Deck.

Nika felt oddly comforted by the simple gesture. As she turned to go, Trisha O'Malley was blocking her path.

The short redhead grinned up at her, "Claudia's a deep one. Guess she likes you. Means the rest of us will too." With a solid punch on the arm—more pain than comfort—the pilot jogged out of the room.

If there was one thing Sly had rammed through her thick skull it was that there was no difference in performance on a training mission versus a live one—if you didn't practice full tilt, you couldn't be sure to deliver full tilt. Within ninety seconds of the strange greeting by the two Night Stalkers, Nika was six decks down, two hundred feet aft, and calling out Sly's typical training line, "Let's go prove we still know how."

"She-it!" was Tom's first comment from where the other three of the crew waited atop the ramp. "Her head is gonna swell something fierce now."

"Might be," Sly replied merrily from close behind her. "Let's find out how badly."

"Ten says her helmet no longer fits," Dave grinned at her.

"Twenty," Tom had to up his buddy of course.

"I'll take both bets," Jerome said quietly in his deep voice.

"No, wait. We were kiddi—"

"Witnessed and signed," Sly called out, siding with Jerome.

"We have to deal with the Army again," Nika went for some control of the situation, "so let's show them how it's done."

"Where are they?" Tom looked up the empty ramp behind Nika and Sly.

Nika pointed east, "Enroute toward Benghazi; which is four hours away."

That quieted the crew, just as it had left Nika mute during the briefing. Carrier Strike Group Two was idling along the Libyan coast out at the extreme range of the LCAC's reach. And that's where they'd been assigned to go. The LCAC could travel five hours on a full fuel load, but was only rarely tasked with a run of more than an hour.

"We leave in three minutes," Nika reached inside the port entry door and grabbed the preflight checklist she always kept hanging there.

Sly stopped her with a hand on her arm and handed her a different checklist, "This is the Craftmaster's." He traded checklists with her, offered a nod of his head and headed off with her Loadmaster's list in hand.

"Chief Stowell."

He stopped and looked back at her call.

"You know what all that means, sailor?"

"I'll muddle through," he flapped the plastic-coated sheet at her then headed off to perform her part of the inspection.

She looked down at the list in her hand and wished she'd told the crew five minutes instead of three. But training had told her that time to action stations should be three minutes, so it would be.

"Tom," she called out as she hurried off. "Get the Well Deck master to open that rear gate. Mama's ready to go play."

"Yes, boss of the swelled head. Marcy," he called up the ramp to the Petty Officer in command of the Well Deck, "let us outta here." Then Dave raced up into the control station to warm up the engines.

At sixty seconds, she had her helmet on—which fit just fine, thank you very much—as the four big engines wound to life. Everyone not on duty had cleared the Well Deck. Those who remained wore double protection—ear plugs and muffs—against the thunder of the big fans the *Peleliu* was running to clear the exhaust fumes of LCAC-316's roaring gas turbines trapped in a steel box.

At two minutes, she'd slid into her Craftmaster seat at the rightmost end of the control console. Thankfully Dave the engineer sat in the middle, because that placed him between her and Tom at navigation. With the intercom connecting their headsets, it didn't really matter, but she appreciated the buffer from Tom's quick humor because he had a tendency to poke your ribs with his elbow to make sure everyone got the joke.

If Sly let her fly both ways today, she'd be seven or eight hours closer to her minimum hour requirement. It wasn't that she wanted to leave Sly's boat, but having a boat of her own would be a sweet treat indeed.

At 2:45 she glanced back at the two seats behind them, the Wave Commander and Troop Commander. On her prior training runs, Sly had perched there.

"Where's the Craftmaster?"

"Wearing your helmet, Petty Officer Maier," Sly called out cheerfully over the intercom.

Wait, she was wearing her helmet… Oh man, right. She was the Craftmaster. Then where was Sly? She leaned forward to look across Dave and Tom over to her usual station forty feet away in the portside turret. Sly waved at her. In the past he'd always borrowed some other petty officer to take the position—Marcy the Well Deck master was cross-trained on the post.

"I don't know, Loadmaster Stowell," Nika said as she did her final checks before departure. "Can I trust you over there by yourself? A lot of responsibility, you know."

"You don't break my boat, Craftmaster Maier, and I'll be fine."

At three minutes to the second, she called out, "Take us up, Dave."

Dave advanced the pitch on the lift propellers and the LCAC raised about three feet off the deck, taking the pressure off the skirt. In that instant, the hovercraft went from a stable vessel moving with the *Peleliu* to an independent, skittery, air hockey puck being bounced off the Well Deck walls by the ship's gentle rocking and the vagaries of the maelstrom unleashed by the big fans operating in an enclosed space.

Easing back on the wheel, LCAC-316 slid slowly back out of the Well Deck. Nika felt the stern of the hovercraft dip as she tipped backward down the steel ramp of the *Peleliu's* rear gate that had been lowered into the sea.

And then, between one eyeblink and the next, she was no longer easing ever so slowly out of a red-lit cavern that roared with the thunder of four jet engines. Instead, she was out on the dark waves.

With a practiced flip of her head, she snapped the night-vision goggles down in front of her eyes and the world went green.

"Heading eight-seven degrees," Tom called out. "Winds at ten knots out of the west for a nice tailwind. Sea state 2; you are cleared for full operating speed."

Sea state 2 meant the biggest wave would barely hit her knee on a beach. The Med was quiet today. The LCAC could fly through waves up to eight feet at full speed, but it wasn't a comfortable ride. This would be like flying on an air hockey table. Sweet!

Nika twisted the wheel and slid it forward. As she picked up speed, the LCAC began to turn to the new heading. Pressing in the rudder control with her left foot, Nika turned the big directable blowers that perched close behind the control station. The ducts pointed off to the side and shoved the bow around faster than the rudders behind the big fan would have. As she came up on the heading, she eased off on the big blowers and slid the wheel the rest of the way forward.

With no load aboard except fuel and the five person crew, ninety tons of LCAC leapt at her command and she shot off into the dark. By the time she thought to look back, the *Peleliu* was little more than a pinprick on the horizon.

This was heaven, even if Jews didn't believe in heaven. It was exactly this.

She wished her side window opened so that she could stick her head out the window and feel the wind. Feel it rip through her hair. It would smell of ocean and freedom. It was all she'd ever wanted.

Well, there was now one thing more that she'd like, but she wasn't going to think about him right now.

# # #

Clint looked down from the helicopter he rode on. The hovercraft raced over the pitch black sea. A cloud of water shot outward in all directions, as if the big craft was floating on a foaming wreath of white spray. Behind it, a long ribbon of ripped waves showed the craft's passage even in his NVGs.

Maybe Nika was right and Clint had too much Santa on the brain. Hanukkah bush, huh? He'd show her a Hanukkah bush and raise her one Christmas spirit. Only problem was where did a man find Jewish tree decorations while flying over the Southern Med?

Actually, another problem: there had to be some way to think of something other than the woman driving the hovercraft racing below. He knew she'd had the training, had seen her drive it before—the slip of a woman and the ninety-ton behemoth. How had he never noticed that before? It was like the girl-driving-a-pickup effect times a thousand.

And then he'd held her and discovered that she felt as neat and compact as she looked. It made their mismatch even more incongruous. But she had also shown him the inner strength that he didn't know she'd had.

That's what had kept him awake the first night. Not that single kiss. It had been good, okay, amazing, but a single kiss didn't alter a man's life; at least it wasn't supposed to in any mission plan he'd ever read. However, discovering that Nika Maier of the Lower East Side of Manhattan had the same spine of steel that Mama had shown in building a great career while raising two kids as a single mom, that had been the eye-opener. He wasn't some guy out looking to find a woman just like his mom. But to discover a woman who embodied the best parts of Lena Barstowe, well, he wasn't going to be laying down any complaints at The Man's door either. Santa was a very wise dude.

The last two weeks had become a blur of discovery and appreciation. They had loved for hours. And when too debilitated to continue, they had talked about everything. How much ground they'd covered how fast was like relationship boot camp. In two weeks with Nika, he knew more about her than he'd ever thought there might be to learn from The Bitch. He—

Damn it! Couldn't he even breath without thinking about her.

Sitting on the outside bench seat of a Little Bird helicopter, racing above dark waves at ninety miles-an-hour, Clint had more view to admire than just the massive craft sliding along a hundred feet below them. Or the lady guiding it. He and Sergeant Lamar sat on the "pod" bench seat mounted on the left-hand side of a Little Bird helicopter, two of his boys sat on the other side, waiting for the maneuver to begin.

His feet dangled over the big nothing, ocean as far as a man could see with only the LCAC hovercraft moving on its dark surface.

On the headset with him was Colonel Gibson sitting in the copilot's seat. They sat close enough together that Gibson's elbow kept bumping the back of Clint's shoulder whenever the Little Bird, flown by his wife Claudia, made a hard maneuver.

"You might want to remain aboard after the exercise," Gibson told him over the intercom without any preamble.

Clint tried to figure out what purpose such a change would make. Gibson hadn't raised the possibility during the briefing. He finally gave up.

"You're going to have to explain that one…" he almost said *Colonel.* But it hadn't sounded like an order. Instead like advice from…a friend? "…Michael," Clint finished lamely after an overlong pause. They'd known each other for a couple of years now, but Clint still found it hard to ease down around the man.

"Knew you were smart," was all Michael said back to him.

Smart? He felt dumber than poor old Rudolph—glued to a bulkhead with a crew of goofballs constantly changing his nose until he didn't know which way was up. He didn't get anything and Colonel Gibson was calling him smart? Wait! Not Colonel. *Michael* Gibson was calling him smart.

That meant…this wasn't about the Army or tonight's maneuver. And Michael wasn't telling him to stay aboard the helicopter, but rather aboard LCAC-316, because that's where he'd be landing as part of this exercise.

Why was it important that he stay aboard? No, he "might want to stay aboard" was what the man had said. Well, he knew one reason that he'd absolutely like to spend the rest of the training mission aboard the LCAC.

Oh. Finally it all made sense. Michael's friendly slap during the briefing had nothing to do with the string of Libyan desert missions nor his team's performance during the terrorist camp takedowns. It had to do with something he'd barely discovered himself.

Make that *someone.*

Clint looked over his shoulder at Michael, but the colonel's attention was focused forward. Perhaps a little too carefully forward. Gibson, who saw everything and understood everything, had seen right through him at the exercise briefing. Perhaps had seen the cheery salute he'd sent Nika's way from the middle of the terrorists' compound two weeks ago and known exactly what was going on, even though Clint had only thought he was teasing Petty Officer Maier at that time.

He knew Gibson respected him, because if he didn't Clint would have found himself reassigned fast enough to make his head spin. And it would be impossible to not respect Nika Maier. If Gibson was thinking to give Clint a nudge as one friend to another, Clint would take that as a good sign.

"Yes, sir," Clint said over the intercom. "That would offer a superior tactical situation. Thank you, sir."

Michael still didn't turn to him, but in his NVGs, Clint thought he saw the Colonel smile.

If his wife—the only other person on the intercom—had a comment, she kept it to herself.

# # #

"Attention 316. Prepare for immediate on-boarding of Ranger team."

"Say what?" Nika stared at the radio in confusion. All she'd been told during the briefing was *Exercise with Rangers and Night Stalkers*. It had seemed so odd that she'd double-checked, but that's all they'd told her.

"A Craftmaster always displays confidence in order to instill same in their crew," Sly spoke it like a beginner's lesson over the intercom. "Especially in rapidly changing scenarios."

"Roger that," Nika keyed the radio. "This is 316. Ranger team is a go." As soon as she was back off the general frequency, she continued over the intercom. "And they call us nuts."

"Incoming," Sly called out.

The words were barely out of his mouth when the LCAC skittered and bucked. A glance over her shoulder and she was looking directly at Captain Claudia Gibson's Little Bird helicopter hovering in the gap between her tower station and Sly's. The helo had two Rangers on bench seats on this side and probably two more on the other.

The blast of air downwashing from the helicopter's rotor blades pounded against the LCAC. They were traveling at seventy miles an hour when the Rangers kicked loose thick fast-ropes; the ends of which hit the hovercraft's deck.

Fast-roping was almost always done on a steady platform with the helicopter in a stable hover. Claudia's helo was nose down, pushing along at half its full-flight speed.

"Rangers away!"

Nika stole a glance to see a Ranger wearing one of their huge field packs slide down from each side, get caught by the wind, and then make it down onto the deck after flapping about like a pair windsocks. As soon as they were clear, two more slid down with nothing but their gloves and their boots to keep them on the whipping rope.

"On the deck!" Clint. She had no trouble recognizing his voice, already it was ingrained. She'd recognize his soft whisper after a kiss or his shout while standing tall in a terrorist camp raid.

The helo released the two fast-ropes, dropping them to the deck, and then raced away over the bow.

The rotorwash drove the LCAC's bow skirt down into a wave and Nika had to compensate, adding extra lift as a wave-load of spray shot over the top of the front gate and doused the Rangers. Served them right for being crazy.

She barely recovered before Trisha O'Malley came in with the next four.

It became a blur.

Four more off another Little Bird.

Then the hammer-load of a dozen Rangers sliding down two ropes off a Black Hawk. The big Sikorsky MH-60M transport bird slapped at her LCAC with ten times the force of the Little Birds. But she'd learned a lot from the line of Little Birds and managed to compensate enough to keep the hovercraft steady under the helicopters.

Five helos blasted her in turn and thirty Rangers hit her deck in under a minute.

No word from any of her crew.

She checked her heading. Still eight-seven degrees true.

They were now thirty Rangers heavy. She was tempted to turn and see if she could spot Clint, but resisted the urge.

"Incoming," Sly called again.

Now what? Nika managed to keep the thought to herself.

Suddenly LCAC-316 bucked like she'd been kicked in the ass.

Nika fought the controls. It was no longer merely a matter of holding her heading. The downwash was now a downblast. She spun the steering blowers until the one on either side pointed out to sea in opposite directions. Feeding power to them kept the hovercraft more tightly trapped on a straight course.

Captain Roberts' massive Chinook MH-47G slid to a hover above her bow and dangled down three long lines.

Then he just sat there.

The LCAC was battered by the pounding wind. Even the little two-foot waves broke hard against the bow despite the fact that she'd pumped all of the lift forward that she could.

A hovercraft was practically frictionless on the surface of the ocean and the twin sixty-foot rotors of the Chinook were doing their best to shove her aside. A shift of even a few feet could be disastrous to the Rangers huddling in the open cargo bay.

Sweat began streaming down her face as she fought to keep her craft steady.

"What are they doing, Sly?"

"Roping up. SPIES extraction."

"SPIES? At sixty knots?" Clint Barstowe wasn't brave, he was completely insane. One false move by her or the Chinook and there'd be little bits of US Rangers scattered all over the LCAC's deck worse than the aftermath of a dinner table at the end of a Passover Seder meal.

"Never seen anything quite like it," Sly's voice was full of wonder.

Sure as hell hadn't been in my training! But she didn't have the spare attention to actually voice that thought. It took everything she had to keep her craft flying true.

Special Patrol Insertion/Extraction System was a fast-rope lowered from a hovering helicopter. On it were ten D-rings embedded through the rope. Rangers always had an extraction clip on their survival vests. They'd snap that into the D-ring on the SPIES rope and then the helo would lift them off the ground. A very fast way to get a team off unfriendly ground without having to land.

But she'd never heard of a full platoon doing it at the same time, and never in seventy miles an hour of wind.

"Someone talk to me," she snarled into the intercom.

"All locked in," Sly reported. "The Rangers all have their arms out to the side."

That was their signal that they were ready to go. The helicopter's crew chief would look down and ensure that every man had their arms out before starting the lift.

"And…there they go. Rope taut. First aloft. Second is up. All three rope teams are off the deck. Damn but that's impressive."

Nika flashed a glance to the side and wished to hell that she hadn't. Thirty US Rangers were being battered about by the wind between her and Sly's lookout stations. If she slipped even a little to the side, she'd have Ranger faces plastered up against her window.

"And…they're clear!" Sly announced.

Nika looked out the front windshield and up as the LCAC settled from the departing Chinook's battering. The helicopter was turning back toward the *Peleliu*. In NVG-green, she could see all of the Rangers flying through the night with their arms still held out to the sides.

"Damn. And I thought we were the crazy ones."

"Told you," Clint's voice came loud and clear on the intercom, "Rangers lead the way."

Nika spun to see Clint sitting in the Troop Commander's seat close behind Dave. He was grinning at her like a lunatic.

"Heading is changing," Tom called out from his navigator's station. "Ninety degrees. One-ten. One-twen—"

"Shut up, Tom!" Nika corrected the LCAC's heading back to eight-seven with a vicious snap that sent her stomach skidding in one direction as 316 twisted in the other.

"A Craftmaster maintains both control of her craft and treats her crew with courtesy."

"You shut up too, Loadmaster Stowell!"

"Anything you say, Craftmaster."

Nika decided on a new policy that would solve any future problems: she was never going to speak to a man again.

Not any of them.

Chapter 9

Clint had found it hard to watch his guys go aloft without him. But the more he'd thought about Gibson's suggestion, the better he'd liked it. Not only for personal reasons, but because it gave him a chance to have his three squad leaders perform a critical task without him hanging over them. Each man was responsible for nine other men which had neatly worked out to be a rope each.

Practically choking on his held breath, he'd forced himself to climb up to the command station and watch as his men did the difficult maneuver without his interference. He hadn't thought of the change until they were all on deck, so it was a chance to observe how adaptable they were on receiving new, last-minute orders. Being good Rangers, they took it in stride and they delivered flawlessly.

He'd been both proud and sick to his stomach.

Nika's statement that Rangers were crazy wasn't news to him. Had to be a little whacko to be one, and more than a little to perform a fast-rope insertion and a SPIES extraction on the deck of a racing LCAC.

But a few minutes later, when his team reported safe back aboard the *Peleliu,* he could finally breathe. Now the debrief and the rest of the night's training would be up to the squad leaders—definitely good practice. And again, he was left with nothing to do but watch.

After the exercise, there was nothing but the soporific calm of the hovercraft skidding over dark ocean. After the adrenal surge let go, it was almost enough to put Clint to sleep. After all, it had been a rare commodity lately.

But watching the smooth confidence of Nika Maier as she guided the craft had the opposite effect. He'd sat in this exact seat on dozens of missions, watching Chief Stowell perform these tasks. While he could see that Nika didn't have his expertise born of long practice, she revealed her own form of smooth grace with every motion.

He barely looked up as they arrived among the vast ships of the carrier strike group. The *George H. W. Bush* never traveled alone. She always had along a trio of destroyers and at least one big cruiser offering protection and heavy firepower. A fast combat supply ship raced about with food, fuel, and ammunition. A pair of fast-attack *Los Angeles* class submarines would also be lurking nearby in a defensive perimeter. Even at night it was a spectacle worth watching, perhaps especially tonight as the carrier air wing was performing night operations. He could hear the jets roaring by, even over the noise of the LCAC itself.

But Clint couldn't drag his attention away from Nika Maier. He was in such deep shit. One kiss was not supposed to warp a man's mind. One meal of teasing each other. An air hockey game which had led to the best sex of his life. Which had led to a dozen nights of heaven and was now bordering on madness.

Damn Gibson for suggesting he stay aboard the LCAC. He really didn't want or need this.

He forced himself to look out at the ships.

There was a strange type of ship in the group. At first, he thought it was a wreck floating close by the resupply ship. All he could see was the tall bow section and far astern the aft section with its command and housing superstructure. Only as Nika brought them closer did he notice that they were connected by a low mid-section. He'd heard of these, modified oil tankers with the tanks and side hulls removed most of the way down to the waterline. In their place lay a low, flat deck—Mobile Landing Platforms.

Sure enough, Nika headed straight at the ship's side. A ramp had been built into the low side of the ship, just the size of an LCAC. She nestled up to it and then eased up the ramp.

Once tucked into place, she nodded to Dave who powered down the engines and the LCAC eased onto the deck. The skirt deflated with a sharp hiss and their forward loading ramp lay down against the flat main deck of the MLP ship. Everyone flipped back their NVGs as the deck lights came on outside the hovercraft. Dave and Tom vacated the cabin as Nika shed her helmet and then did a long slow stretch that made him ache to run his hands over her.

It was only then that he realized he hadn't heard a single radio call in the whole maneuver. He'd seen Nika's lips moving, but not heard a word.

"You cut me out of the intercom."

Nika looked over at him, her brown eyes bright with light from the MLP ship's deck lights shining in through the control station's windows.

"About an hour ago, Army. You may lead the way, but you're too goddamn distracting."

He considered being offended at the cutout, but he liked her reason. "Distracting you, am I?"

Her curse was soft and very unladylike.

"Music to my ears, Navy."

She clambered out of her seat. Despite her being a full-size smaller than him or her crew, the control station was still a very cramped space. After four hours in the chair, she was shrugging shoulders and weaving her neck side to side.

"Turn around."

Nika glared at him. His observer seat was high enough that they were eye to eye.

"Can't you do anything without making it a thing, woman?" But he already knew the answer to that so he didn't bother waiting for it. He grabbed her by the shoulders and turned her around.

When she tried to step away, he simply trapped her hips between his knees and tried not to think lustful thoughts as Nika had a very fine stern section that even the blue-gray camouflage of her Naval Working Uniform couldn't do anything to hide. Then he clamped his hands on her shoulders and dug his thumbs into the soft muscle tissue between her spine and shoulder blades.

"Ow, cut that out! Ow. Ow! Hey, ow!!"

Not quite the groan of pleasure he'd been counting on.

"Damn it, Barstowe. I'm not a goddamn Ranger," she almost managed to drag her shoulders out of his grasp, would have if not for the grip of his knees.

He eased way back. He'd been thinking of digging in the way you did when a Ranger cramped up bad and you couldn't delay the hike. A fast, hard, deep massage to break up the muscle knot would be in order, and then back on the move. Massaging a woman was new to him. He didn't even know why he'd started and he almost stopped.

But he wanted to touch her so badly that he decided to just keep going, but softer. He traced the line of her shoulder blades, finding muscle knots the size of his fingertip, not Ranger-sized ones in calf or thigh muscles as big as his bunched fist. He nudged them more carefully and they slowly gave way. After he loosened the third one he felt he was getting the hang of it.

Nika braced her hands against the back of Dave's chair and hung her head forward. Her soft groan filled the small cabin and confirmed that he was finally on the right track.

"You taking advantage of my Petty Officer, Lieutenant Barstowe?" The sharp tone in Sly's voice startled him. He looked at the Chief who was halfway up the ladder into the control station.

He had no idea how to respond. He had Nika Maier's hips pinned between his knees and his big hands on her shoulders. Had even held her there when she'd tried to pull away. But he wasn't…

"Go away, Sly," Nika gasped out. "If you make him stop, I'm gonna tell your wife that you always add ketchup to her food when she isn't watching." The high tomato content of Sly's North Carolina barbeque sauce had been a hotly contested point in their courtship.

"But I don't," Sly protested.

"I'll tell her anyway. It's not my fault you married the most talented Chief Steward in the Navy. Now go away."

Clint did his best not to look too obvious about removing his hands and unclamping his knees from her hips.

A glance at Sly showed the grim expression was gone… mostly. Clint knew that he and Sly were going to be having some words in the near future.

"Got a loading issue you'll want to take a look at, Craftmaster." Sly's tone was painfully formal and he wasn't looking at Clint even a little. No friendly joking tone about his and Nika's change in roles; not with the evil Army lieutenant who had his hands all over one of Chief Stowell's crew.

"Roger that," Nika replied.

Sly eyed Clint carefully one more time before dropping back down the ladder and going away. Clint would bet not very far away.

"Sorry," Clint mouthed.

Nika turned without stepping out from between his knees. Not saying a word, she leaned in to kiss him. This time he was one who was paralyzed, unable to even raise his hands to her waist. His big hands couldn't fully circle it, because she wasn't that kind of petite. But they'd certainly felt good there.

Her skilled hands that had guided the LCAC so skillfully, slid onto his chest and rested there. She leaned in until their lips were just brushing. A test. A taste. A nuzzle.

Between that soft moment and the next instant, she shifted, as if he was suddenly kissing a different woman. She drove her mouth hard enough against his that he banged the back of his head on the control station's rear window. A gentle brush turned into a flaming French kiss with such a startling suddenness that even his Ranger-trained reactions didn't stand a chance of shifting fast enough.

"There," she stepped back. "That should screw with your head for a while. Paybacks are hell, aren't they, soldier?" She looked indecently pleased with herself.

After a long heartbeat of continued paralysis, he lunged for her. His seatbelt kept him attached to his seat.

"Put your hat back on, Ranger."

Clint hadn't even noticed her brushing it aside. He seated it back firmly on his head.

"Damn but you're just too cute," then she disappeared down the ladder.

Clint wasn't sure how he felt, as a Ranger, about being called "cute." He reached up and pulled off his Santa hat. He turned it over and over in his hands, looking at it.

She still hadn't kissed "the man in the hat" despite his prediction. But he'd gotten far more than he'd bargained for this holiday season. He couldn't believe what he was thinking, but the next time they were alone together, it was going to be about way more than body-numbing sex...not that he was going to fight against that either. Next time it was going to be about making love. Because that's exactly what he was feeling.

Then Clint looked out the window and what he saw had him scrabbling against his seatbelt to get down on deck.

# # #

Nika was looking up at the three vehicles rolling down from the supply ship and didn't like them one little bit. The big ship had a hangar-sized opening high on its side. The Mobile Landing

Platform ship had a massive ramp almost as long as its deck on hydraulic jacks. One end of it had been raised so that the line of three vehicles simply drove off the supply ship, down the ramp as if it was a highway exit, and onto the main deck of the MLP. It was an impressive operation.

It was the third vehicle that was bothering her, that and the specs that Sly had handed her without comment. All three were ugly as sin and looked just as dangerous, but she was used to that in military vehicles. The more they were adapted for IED attacks, the uglier they became. That wasn't the problem. That the third one was a military ambulance was a major issue.

Now she looked at the loading specification sheets that she held in one hand—fourteen-tons-per-vehicle, forty-two tons all combined. That at least explained why they hadn't used Captain Roberts' Chinook for the run; it was a massive heavy-lift helicopter, but topped out around twelve tons.

Worse, behind the three M-ATVs was a general supplies container with another twenty tons of foodstuffs and ammunition restock. All together they totaled the same as an M1A2 Abrams main battle tank, the hovercraft's upper limit except under emergency conditions.

"Gee, thanks, Chief," Nika couldn't help giving Sly some flak. Getting full capacity loads exactly right were a real pain. Unlike a tank, she had four different objects with two different centers of gravity. They could be arranged a dozen different ways and the challenge was to make sure that it was perfectly distributed across the deck of the LCAC or she wouldn't fly right. Classic Navy thinking, maximum load at maximum range capability. Not the MLP's problem, it was hers.

When Sly didn't respond, she turned to look at him.

He wasn't looking at her. He was glaring at Clint.

Clint in turn was oblivious to both of them. He was staring at the approaching vehicles but his reaction was very different from her own. He looked at them as if the MLP was indeed

Santa's sleigh and it had just brought him the most beautiful of presents.

"Oh baby," he moaned softly in a way she recognized only too well. "Come to Pappy!"

It was really too bad Sly was standing there. If he hadn't been, Clint might find himself going for a night swim in the Mediterranean. As it was, she could tell that she needed to keep these two men as carefully separated on the hovercraft as the equipment they were about to load.

All that would be okay, if it wasn't for the report that she held in her other hand. That was the one presently freaking her out.

A storm was forming up over Central Libya and was probably going to catch up with them before they reached the *Peleliu*. Staying with the MLP and the carrier strike group wasn't an option as they were headed to the mess in the eastern Med as soon as they were rid of her.

# # #

"What's the big deal?" Clint couldn't believe what he was hearing. "God, you really are a swabbie, Maier." He couldn't stop looking down at his pretty new vehicles from the control station as Nika eased them back out onto the ocean.

"Careful there, Lieutenant. Your *Pappy* wouldn't be amused." Her tone was neutral, but he felt as if he'd just been slapped.

She'd been acting strangely ever since he'd met her down on the loading deck. Had Sly said something to her? That didn't seem likely.

Not knowing what minefield he'd just wandered into, he decided to proceed more carefully.

"Those," he said over the intercom, waving his hand toward the vehicles now chained to the hovercraft's deck even though he knew Nika couldn't see him do so. "Imagine that the Ranger Special Operations Vehicles that we drove into the terrorist camp are Land Rovers on steroids. These are Humvees on steroids. An

RSOV is rated as a light tactical vehicle and an IED can make a real mess of it and the guys on board. M-ATV stands for MRAP All-Terrain Vehicle. Mine resistant ambush protected, it can cross through man-deep water or climb a sixty percent grade. All while delivering seven Rangers and a turret-mounted heavy machine gun. It's a sweet deal."

"What about the third one?" She had them turned west and had opened up the throttle. The roar echoed right down to his bones.

"The EXM? Extraction-medical. Probably won't need it, at least not as long as we have the Night Stalkers watching over us. Still, always nice to be prepared." Was that it? Was she worried about him being hurt? Seemed odd. After four tours, even Navy, she'd know that their chosen profession wasn't the safest one around. But it was a profession that made perfect sense to him.

He'd joined the Army because he enjoyed the structure and had found the male camaraderie that had been lacking elsewhere. He'd been in long enough that now he was being a father figure to some of the guys with backgrounds way more messed up than his own. Which was pretty great as he never expected to have kids himself.

Whereas Nika…

He looked at the back of her helmet as she flew them into the roughening weather. He suddenly realized that he still had no idea why she served. Their boot camp relationship had covered a lot of terrain, but somehow it had missed that one point. It was odd, it was usually the first thing a grunt talked about. He hadn't pushed since her initial harsh reaction, but it was time. He really wanted to know; maybe even needed to know.

Then he glanced out the window to where Sly rode in Nika's normal spotter position across the hovercraft. He wasn't happy with Clint either. Perhaps he could understand that. Sly wouldn't know that it was mutual between them.

He considered moseying over there to chat with Sly, reassure him. Sure, reassure his best friend about his intentions toward his friend's best crew member—when Clint didn't know what the hell his real intentions were anyway.

There was a plan designed to fail.

A big sheet of spray shot over the bow. Another good reason to wait.

# # #

"Talk to me, Chief." They were two hours out from the MLP and close to three from the *Peleliu,* and it wasn't going well.

"Go ahead, Craftmaster."

Nika cursed, hopefully too softly for the intercom to pick up. "Can we cut the Craftmaster crap, Chief?"

"No. As long as you are at the controls, you have command. She's your ship."

Figured.

She had an Army Ranger who she'd finally noticed had been granted far too easy access to her emotions. And seeing that damned military ambulance had driven home just how deep that access went. Nika was also a long way from deciding whether it was comforting or embarrassing or pissing her off having him sit so close behind her and watch every move.

Now she also had a commander who was insisting she was in command and the situation was getting ugly. There was a damned storm pounding on *her* command.

"Well, *my* baby is getting the crap beat out of her." Even as she said it, another wave hammered the port quarter. Sly's station disappeared behind a wall of spray.

The storm had formed far faster than even the most pessimistic predictions. The cold desert air had been rushed out to sea by a major high pressure zone moving north out of central Africa. When it hit the relatively warm air of the southern Med, it had hashed up a whole series of squall lines. Those dumped buckets of rain on them—big ones—in addition to the sheets of blinding spray even bigger than usual aboard an LCAC.

The storm had built up from the southwest and overrun the *Peleliu's* position. The problem was, they had to drive southwest to return to their ship—straight into the storm. Hard enough work for any boat, but brutally difficult in a craft that wasn't supposed to actually touch the water.

Her visibility was zero-zero despite the high-speed wipers, and her sense of up and down was going. The storm had thrashed the Mediterranean into sea state 4. The waves were running eight-plus feet already. She'd reduced speed, but it was still a battle.

"So tell me what your plan is," Sly told her.

"Hand off the controls to you."

"Not much of a plan, Craftmaster. I have no better answers on this than you do."

She cursed under her breath. She'd really hoped that he did.

"Tom, what's the distance back to the carrier group?"

"Farther than it is to the *Peleliu*. And at the rate they're steaming east, you won't catch them before fuel zero. So, unless you want to turn around an entire carrier strike group, you'll need another solution."

Nika glared out at the darkness for a long moment, trying to twist the hovercraft sharply enough to take the next wave head on. Not having a keel made one approach to the big waves as bad as any other. There was a gut-wrenching slap as the impact sent them skidding sideways.

She hit the radio, "USS *Peleliu*, this is LCAC-316. Over."

"*Peleliu*. Go ahead, 316."

"Request current sea state your position, predicted for next two hours, and how soon can you make max speed toward our position."

"316. Are you declaring an emergency?"

"Not yet. Just get me the information and do it fast."

It was a long minute before the operator came back.

"Sea state 6 our location. Predicted to remain at six to seven for the next seven hours. You are still two hundred miles out, eight hours at our best speed. Please be advised, that will not outrun the leading edge of the storm which will continue to build in your present position for another three hours." She'd have whimpered, but that wasn't what the commander of a Navy vessel did, especially in front of an Army soldier.

"Chief," she called over to Sly. "You've driven these a lot longer than I have. What are our chances fully loaded in twenty to thirty foot seas?"

Nika didn't need his one word response to know the answer to that one. And even if they could get through it, there would be no way to reboard the ship—entering the Well Deck was a dicey operation under the best of circumstances.

"If we could get the MLP ship to turn back to the east," Sly's voice was hesitant over the intercom, "that would give us a good chance of reaching them. Of course we'd do better if we could lighten up by dumping this load."

"What? No! You can't do—"

""Shut up, Lieutenant!" Nika snapped at Clint.

It was the first time he'd spoken to her since the brief exchange about the M-ATVs. Clint was a tip-of-the-spear kind of guy. It suited him and she couldn't imagine him as anything less. But his taking delivery of an armored ambulance with an M240 turret-mounted machine gun had been a wakeup call that she hadn't been ready for.

She didn't like being scared for another's life—she'd been done with that the day Keila killed herself. Shock, anger, and grief all in one jumbled blast—easier just to shut it out and be done with it. Nika needed time to think how she felt about caring again; how she felt about Clint. Now wasn't it. She had a ship and a crew to save.

Nika considered the suggestion. Three M-ATVs. Million and a half dollars. That would take a mess of paperwork to explain. Worse, the Loadmaster part of her couldn't calculate how to do that without causing a temporarily unbalanced load that would drive the LCAC into the sea. Out the stern gate would be the only possibly survivable option, but she had positioned the supplies container at the very stern. She doubted whether the M-ATVs could move that, even if someone was crazy enough to try driving them in order to ram a container overboard without going overboard themselves.

"Don't think we can do that without heaving to…" Nika left the statement open.

There was a long pause before Sly filled it in, "…which isn't something I'd like to try in this weather." It was possible to sink an LCAC. Allowing heavy seas to break aboard by stopping and settling onto the surface while unshipping a maximum load would be a very efficient way to achieve that.

Which left them only one option.

"Tom, what's my nearest landfall?"

"Libya."

"Try again."

"Seriously, Nika. That's about the best I've got."

Nika wished she could take the time to glare over at him. Of course the cabin was dark and it was well past midnight in a growing storm, so there wouldn't be much to see. She filed the glare away for later usage.

"We're out in the middle of the Med," Tom continued. "Libya is about a hundred and fifty miles from our present position to the south and southeast, and we have two hundred miles of fuel in the tanks. It's within range."

"Quartering across the headwind of a worsening storm for two to three hours in order to land on hostile shores," Nika didn't like the sound of that at all.

Tom didn't answer her back and she rather wished he would.

Chapter 10

Nika fought the controls of the bucking hovercraft like a champion, but Clint didn't see how this was going to end up any way good. He kept looking down at his new vehicles and feeling eight kinds of a fool. Of course equipment was expendable in an emergency. And now that he was starting to understand the full extent of the emergency, Clint agreed that his own skin was more valuable than the M-ATVs.

Having already earned Nika's ire once, he hesitated before speaking. But he had an idea, so he went for it.

"Worst case scenario, we could ask the Night Stalkers to come out and perform another SPIES extraction."

Nika's long silence worried him. How thoroughly had he pissed her off?

"That sounds little better than the Libyan coast," thankfully her tone was thoughtful when she finally spoke. "I don't want to lose any of it: the load or the hovercraft."

That was a relief.

"Or our lives," Tom's attempt at cheer fell flat, which made Clint appreciate Tom a bit more because Clint had been about to say the same thing and was now glad he hadn't.

"What if…" he had another idea. Or the edge of one.

"Spit it out, Army."

Clint looked out at the storm for several seconds before continuing. He was seeing a different scene than the storm-tossed ocean. He pictured instead that desert terrorist camp.

"Lieutenant…" Nika's patience was wearing thin.

There it was. "Come from the unexpected direction! Turn around. What's the nearest landfall if we run away from the storm?"

There was a silence as Tom scrambled around on his electronic maps. The radar screen was covered by a wide tube facing Tom so that it could be used in bright sunlight. Clint leaned so that he could see parts of the screen past Tom's helmet. He was scrolling far and wide.

Not looking good.

"Four hundred miles northwest to Malta."

"No good," Clint answered. "Storm is out of the southwest and that's broadside to it. We need to run roughly northeast. What's the closest downwind?"

"All I've got is Crete."

"Crete?" Nika sounded startled. "As in southern Greece? How far is that?"

"Also four hundred miles," Tom's voice was a death knell. He'd already said that there was only fuel for two hundred miles. Even his typical volubility didn't find that to be worth repeating.

Clint shifted the last step of the way into soldier mode. No ship to fetch them, no land to be reached, they were in it. Chances of the hovercraft going down were high. Now, just as it was in battle, it was a matter of survival. Calm. Panic had long since been trained out of him.

He twisted around and looked out the window. He could just see the outline of the life raft container close behind the control station. There was another on the far side that Sly could get to without crossing the deck.

Clint began mapping out the best routes for abandoning the ship in his head. Priority, make sure that the much lighter Petty Officer Maier wasn't swept away by a rogue wave during the process. Even the spume that the wind was now ripping off the wave tops would be a hazard to her. Then—

Nika slammed the controls over. Between one wave and the next—the broad side of the hovercraft sliding steeply up the face of a wave, then racing back into the trough—they were flying east.

The ride—which had been doing its best to snap Clint's neck with its whiplash impacts against each wave—smoothed out a little.

"What the hell, Maier?" Tom shouted over the intercom. "We have less than half the fuel we need to reach Crete."

"What are my tailwinds?"

"Not enough."

"Answer the god damn question, Trambley." If Clint had thought there was heat in her voice when she'd told him to shut up, he'd been mistaken. That had just been Nika irritated. Now she was a Craftmaster and ready to eviscerate anyone being less than perfect. Curiously, he didn't hear The Rage. She'd been right; when on duty she was a hundred percent under control.

"Thirty knots. Gusts peaking at fifty."

"Lieutenant."

"Yo!" He responded before he even had time to process that she was calling on him. In the Craftmaster's seat, Nika Maier had found a tone of command that he didn't know she'd had.

"How much fuel is in the M-ATVs?"

"Full," then he knew that wasn't what she needed. "A hundred and twenty gallons combined, plus another thirty in the strap-on cans."

"That buys us ten more minutes of flight time. A dozen miles at our present speed." He kept forgetting how like an airplane this craft was. It burned a thousand gallons per hour and made his contribution practically meaningless.

"It's diesel," he reminded her. "Your engines will burn it, but they won't like it."

"Okay. Hold that in reserve."

Turned east and downwind through the storm, they were now moving faster than the waves. Instead of being slapped by ramming into the steep, breaking side of the waves, they were rocketing off the backs of the waves as if they were ski jumps. Fully loaded, Maier was skittering a hundred and eighty tons through the air like a freestyle skier. He finally understood how she'd beat him at air hockey—she was just that damn good. As good as Colonel Gibson in her own way.

He looked once more out at the vehicles, helpless to assist. That's when he noticed that one of the chains had broken free on the medical M-ATV. If that shifted unduly, it could unbalance the whole craft.

"Jerome," Clint called over the headset. "Meet me on deck. Bring a fresh chain." He popped loose his seatbelt and was reaching for the intercom cable to his helmet when he heard Nika's voice.

"You be damned careful out there, Clint." It was the first time she'd actually used his name. Even in all of their lovemaking and conversation it was always Army this or soldier that. He took the change as a very positive sign to which he could only think of one appropriate response.

"Hoo-ah!"

He was a US Ranger after all.

# # #

Nika would have snorted with laughter if she wasn't so scared for him. The irony was immense. She'd been worried about him being carried off some hypothetical battlefield by an EXM ambulance; now, if he wasn't careful, he could be killed by one.

The fear wrenched in her gut so deeply that it hurt and forced her to bend over the steering wheel as she struggled to get her breath back.

Why?

Was it so hard to imagine a world without him?

She had eased back to the most efficient fuel-per-distance speed, but the waves were still up near the limit for the fully-loaded LCAC. She considered easing off further, to make the work on the deck safer, but if she did there wasn't a chance of her fuel lasting.

As it was, she was betting on the leading edge of the storm continuing to shove them east toward Crete almost as fast as she was driving. At a combined speed nearing a hundred miles an hour...she still wasn't going to make it.

"*Peleliu*. This is 316," she called over the radio.

"Go ahead 316."

"I need to talk to Chief Warrant Lola Maloney."

While she waited for them to track her down, Nika felt well and truly trapped. After hours of hectic driving, loading, and fighting the storm on the return journey, Nika now had nothing to do but continue to seek the smoothest path she could find and hope that Clint and Jerome survived their excursion out onto the deck.

The image of Clint lying close above her, his eyes practically rolled back in his head as he gasped against the pleasure he took from her body, had occupied far too much of her thoughts.

Two weeks. Tomorrow was two weeks...assuming they lived that long. Two weeks was good. It was fun. In two weeks with the few men she kept that long, the sex and the relationship were already becoming predictable. Within a week they'd shown everything they had to offer, by two weeks it had reached that steady state that was never going to go any higher no matter how long they were together.

Two weeks with Clint Barstowe and it felt as if they hadn't even reached the Flight Deck, never mind launched off the safety of the ship. If she spent three weeks with him, she'd never find her way back out.

Done.

They had to be done. It was the only way out.

Her heart had survived this long by never again becoming attached to someone—the immense first blow had been losing her friend, more like her sister, and that had been one blow too many. If she did get attached to Clint, and then lost him, her heart would shatter. Better to float along as she always had.

Petty Officer, someday Chief.

LCAC Loadmaster, someday Craftmaster. Graduate to the SSC ship-to-shore connector when they got the LCAC replacement running.

She'd never live up to Keila's potential. Straight-A student. Navy ROTC. Officer-in-the-making.

Nika was none of those and knew it the day she signed up, so she didn't aspire to be more than she was. But she worked hard and did as well as she could. As Keila had been lowered into the cold ground of Mount Zion Cemetery in Queens, it was what Nika had promised her friend she would do. Work hard. That same day she'd also promised herself that she'd never again care so much about another person. To her mother, a promise was merely another weapon in her arsenal of guilt. In reaction, Nika had never broken a promise in her life.

A rogue cross-wave rose out of the night. She risked a sharp twist of the LCAC. Better for her people on deck to stumble and fall from the unexpected motion than have a wave ram aboard and slam them into the bulwarks.

She paid for it when one of the engines swallowed a gutful of seawater.

"Number three out," Dave Newcomb announced from close beside her. "Restarting."

She counted beats and used the rudders and blowers to compensate for the slowing rear pusher propeller on the starboard side.

"Restart failed. Restarting," Dave remained calm, working his engine controls. It was how they were all trained to be in any emergency.

The hovercraft's sideways slew across the waves was getting harder and harder to compensate for. She hit the switch for the ship's PA, "Caution on deck. Imminent bow wave over gate."

Just as she'd anticipated, the hovercraft nosed hard into the next crossing wave and there was nothing she could do about it. A sheet of green water curled high over the gate and crashed aboard.

"Tom? We still have them?" He was seated against the window overlooking the deck.

"Roger that. Three on deck."

"Pumps running well," Dave reported as he continued working the engine.

Three? Sly, of course.

Odd that Sly hadn't caught on to what was happening between her and Clint. He had now, though. She'd have to tell Sly to let it go...right after she told Clint they were done.

She sighed. Neither conversation was going to go well.

"Restart successful," Dave slowly worked the engine back up to speed and fed her the power to straighten out the hovercraft.

If only it was so easy with the men.

# # #

Clint was soaked to the bone. His flightsuit for the fast-rope landing he'd done an infinity ago was not a diver's dry suit. It wasn't a wet suit either, though he was certainly soaked enough for it to be.

He, Jerome, and Sly had anchored each other in place and finally managed to replace the broken chain. Then Jerome had worked them around each vehicle until every chain was checked and tightened. Staggering like drunks due to the Tilt-A-Whirl motion of the hovercraft and the battering of the waves, the job had taken them over an hour. By then even Clint's underwear was a squidgy mess from the cold seawater that had sloshed past his collar and run all down his back.

He and Sly huddled around the heater in the portside cabin. Jerome had gone up to sit in the portside lookout, not that there was a damn thing for him to see and report—it was still pitch black and nasty out there. They'd worn headlamps that had done little to cut the night, but the full deck lights would have blinded Nika. As they'd fought the battle, he'd taken comfort from the occasional glimpses of her sitting steadfast at the controls.

"So, Sly, this is what you guys do for entertainment? Maybe the Navy really is crazier than the Rangers."

"Keeps us out of trouble, Clint."

"Where's the fun in that?"

But Sly wasn't joking around. Had he been more battered by the waves than he'd let on? Or…oh. Clint decided it was definitely "Or" and figured he'd better tackle the subject head on himself.

"Two weeks, Sly." That's how long Nika Maier had been letting him come to her bed.

"How the hell did I miss that?"

"She doesn't talk much, does she?" He was particularly chagrined as he'd thought about it more while fighting the storm. Nika had told him all about things she had done, but never about anything she felt. A chasm-sized hole that he'd been too happy screwing her to notice. The more he'd thought about it, the vaster her silence had become.

"Quick with a joke, but otherwise, no, not much," Sly rubbed at his face with hands as large as Clint's own. It reminded him of the Army-Navy wrestling match aboard the *Peleliu* that had started their friendship. A match that Sly had won, though Clint had definitely made him work for it. Until Delta Colonel Michael Gibson had wiped the mats with Sly seconds later, which had helped Clint feel a little better about losing.

"She's really something, Sly. I understand that." Really something? She was making him reevaluate his whole never-trust-another-woman rule.

"You forget it for a single second and you'll have me to deal with. We clear on that?"

"Crystal." Clint didn't point out that if he pissed off Nika, there probably wouldn't be much left of him for Sly to take apart. They sat together in a silence that eventually became companionable as their body chill receded beneath the heater's blast.

As they dried out, Clint got to thinking about the woman on the other side of the boat. Sure, he knew she was something special; he'd never had a lover like her. But that wasn't all of it—wasn't even the half or a quarter of what had snared him about her.

She'd taken a training run exercise that had turned into a storm and stayed strong right through the heart of it. He'd observed her closely these last few weeks, and not only because she was such a joy to watch.

Every person she dealt with on a regular basis respected her immensely. Jerome, her assistant Loadmaster, practically worshipped the ground she walked on. Or perhaps the sea she flew on.

He'd talked to Lamar and Jeffries, the two RSOV drivers. They too were as impressed as hell by LCAC-316's Loadmaster. And then Sly had refused to take back the controls during the storm and Clint knew why. Sly was a good enough leader to know when one of his crew only needed a little seasoning to become truly superior. Maybe Sly knew a few other things about her. He decided to start off with a tease.

"Nika flies this thing like a dream."

Sly nodded.

"You fearing for your job, buddy? She's way cuter than you too. Hell, she's cuter than a boxful of puppies, though she'd kill me if she heard that. If it was between the two of you and it was me doing the picking, I'd sure—"

"Incoming!" Jerome dropped down the ladder. "Friendly! Craftmaster says to get back out there."

"Shit!" The hovercraft was still slamming over the waves. He scrambled out of the cabin on Jerome and Sly's heels and instantly caught of faceful of cold sea spray. Then he almost cried out when the big Chinook helicopter slipped down low above them.

It was dangling a long line out of its rear cargo ramp as it hovered a hundred feet above them. The down blast from the rotors momentarily pinned him back against the side of the cabin.

Had Nika called for a SPIES extraction after all?

But it wasn't a rope. It was a wire with a big clip on the end.

"Don't touch it," Jerome shouted out.

Clint dove to the deck as the cable whipped sideways and the clip hit the cabin right where his head had been. The sharp clang of impact was nearly drowned out by the loud *Pow!* of a spark that lit up the immediate area of the deck like a lightning bolt.

Then Jerome grabbed the cable and shouted, "Static discharge from the rotors."

Clint knew that, and was glad it had missed him. He'd taken a full body shock from a winch cable before and it wasn't fun.

But instead of a snap ring for lifting out crew, it looked more like a spring clip for jumping a battery.

Jerome snapped it onto a piece of the LCAC's hull. Then a hose snaked down from the hovering helicopter. A fuel hose. Christ! Fueling was the most dangerous operation anywhere. Doing it from an airborne platform down to a storm-tossed hovercraft was the craziest damn thing he'd ever seen.

Sly had the fueling port open. Jerome twisted the hose onto the locking ring just as another wave slammed into them.

Clint managed to get a handhold on both a deck tie-down and Jerome's life vest. He held on for all he was worth until the water had run down and back out the scuppers.

"Begin fueling!" Jerome shouted over the radio once he'd spit out enough water to speak. The hose snapped from flat to round as fuel rushed down to them from the hovering helo.

Clint glanced up at the control station.

Tom was watching them closely. All he could see of Nika was the back of her helmet as she continued to pay attention forward, but it was enough. He'd know her anywhere.

And in that moment, he knew that was a feeling he wanted to have for the rest of his life.

# # #

Nika was ragged by the time they spotted land. Another storm front had swept south out of Italy along the Adriatic Sea and collided with the one headed northeast across the Ionian Sea. The two collided right over their position.

With the fifteen hundred gallons she'd grabbed from the Chinook helicopter before Captain Roberts had to wave off, both Italy and Greece were technically possible, but not through this storm. Any thoughts of turning about and fighting back upwind toward the *Peleliu* were shut down when Lola Maloney ordered Roberts to continue on to Izmir Air Base in Turkey rather than return to the ship. The sea state around the ship hadn't slackened and there was some doubt whether the big Chinook could land safely back aboard in this weather.

What had it taken to launch from such a pitching platform? It had taken a Night Stalker. She was damned lucky to serve with such amazing people.

She was shooting for Crete, but even that landfall was getting dicey.

"Gavdos," Tom called out. "We can land on Gavdos Island in ten minutes. Crete is still thirty minutes beyond that."

She didn't know if she had thirty more minutes of fuel, or ten for that matter. They were down to fumes now. Just as she was. Lack of sleep, lack of caffeine, and all of the hours on high alert, she didn't know what she had left in her.

The new storm was still driving her from behind when she first spotted the island.

"Cliffs, Tom. Cliffs and more cliffs. How am I supposed to—" she clamped down on her tongue because she was that close to losing it completely.

"Around the south end. Cape Tripiti. I'd stay well out to sea, it looks nasty on the map. There's a beach named Aliki around the back side that should be out of the wind."

"Aliki Beach by Cape Tripiti," she muttered to herself. "Coney Island in Brooklyn. Now that's a beach."

A wave batted her into a sideways skid and she cursed as she reoriented the craft. Dave had given her half a dozen different warnings: temperature this, pressure that, strain the other. They were held together with spit and bailing wire.

"Give me a Nathan's cheese dog and crinkle-cut chili fries. That's what you're supposed to have on a beach, not hour seven of a god damn storm!" She leaned forward to yell the last of it up at the sky.

Stars. There were stars here. The waves and wind were murder, but there were stars.

"Approaching Cape Tripiti," Tom called out, his voice carefully neutral.

"Shit!" She was approaching it head on.

The cape was a long crag of rock that reached well out from shore at the very southern tip of the island which made it the southernmost point of all of Europe. The sea had punched great arches through the headland. She was half tempted to see if she could race through the big one without a wave smashing her against the top of it.

Instead, she swung wide around the headland and turned for the beach. It faced east, away from the storm, and was set back in a cove. The waves here were smaller but terribly confused. No clean surf line to ride ashore.

"No wakeboarding today, campers."

None of the crew answered her.

She picked her line, gave the hovercraft maximum lift and slowed to ease ashore. After the hours racing over the ugly sea that was always in motion, the unmoving shore was approaching deceptively fast. Nika was at best approach speed, but the land looked unreal and dangerous after so long on the waves.

The beach had a shallow slope, which was a good thing.

She reached up and hit the big landing lights.

"Damn it!" She slammed her eyes shut and shoved the night-vision goggles out of her way. Still she saw spots from that hugely amplified glare.

Mostly blind, she rolled out of the heavy surf and, with a hard jolt, cushioned by all the air two jet engines run to redline could produce and blow downward, she hit the beach.

"Cobble beach. Not even decent sand like Coney Island."

The LCAC continued to meander inland.

Moments later she was over water again.

What the—?

Oh.

A broad lake just at the back of the beach. A lagoon.

A hundred yards later there was land again…a path… goat-wide…she started to follow it until a few scrub trees to one side and a large boulder to the other stopped the progress of her fifty-foot wide hovercraft.

"Ease it down, honey," a nice deep voice wrapped around her. "You got us here."

She slid the steering wheel to neutral.

Dave pulled back on the throttles between their positions and the hovercraft settled.

Shut down. She should be telling someone to shut down… but they already were…she was…shutting down.

"Come on, honey." That warm voice again. "Let's get you out of that seat." Strong hands released her and swept her up effortlessly.

Nika curled against that wonderful chest that she'd come to know so well.

She was really going to miss that chest.

# # #

"Why did you push her like that?" Clint felt as ragged as Nika looked. She was passed out on the starboardside cabin floor cocooned in blankets, her face pale with exhaustion as the storm roared outside almost as loudly as the now silent LCAC's engines.

Sly didn't glare at him or snarl back as Clint deserved.

Instead he simply looked down at his sacked out petty officer.

"You're a Ranger, Clint. You know about training past limits."

He did, and that was more effective than any snarl. Clint was arguing with a man he liked and trusted about the training methods he was using on his own crew. And Sly was right.

Much of Ranger training was about discovering what actually was possible, rather than what he had *thought* he could do. A 10k hike with a full pack? How about twenty-five? Or lead a team? No problem. Through a swamp when he hadn't slept in so long that it was hard to tell if he was hallucinating whether or not there was a map in front of him? He'd learned he could do that too.

"Petty Officer Maier," Sly's tone was surprisingly soft, "has never reached a limit. Last night is the worst I've ever left her to face. Think about what she learned about her own capabilities; a whole new yardstick. And, honest truth, I don't know if I could have done as well. That's the other reason I didn't take over."

"I recall that we had some work to do ourselves. I'm just as glad it wasn't her out on that deck. That was harsh."

His comment earned him a slow smile. The two of them and Jerome would be sporting bruises for weeks from the battering they'd taken doing the deck work while underway. The hourly patrol of the tie-down chains had become a near constant battle which kept them out in the bitter weather effecting some repair or other so that Nika had a functioning craft to fight the storm with.

Then Clint looked down at Nika and tried not to think about the way she'd clung to him once he'd extracted her from the Craftmaster's seat and then gone unexpectedly limp in his arms. A whole new type of panic had swamped him until he'd been able to verify that she was still breathing. He'd handed her below, then they'd wrapped her in blankets. Without the engines running, there was no heat. So he'd pulled his Santa cap down over her ears until only her eyes and nose were showing between the hat and the blankets. Still she looked like a merry elf, just a very tired one.

"Damn woman has gotten all the way under my skin."

"That problem," Sly raised bloodshot eyes to look at him, "that's one I know all about." He raised his left hand and tapped his thumb against his wedding ring.

Clint had already been there once. But his stated intention of never going back there sounded downright stupid now. Looking at the sleeping Nika Maier, he couldn't imagine not asking her to marry him some day. Some day soon. Which was impossible, but that didn't make it any less true.

Though he hadn't said a word, Sly studied him through narrowed eyes.

Clint looked straight back at him and answered the unspoken question, "I've second guessed a lot of choices in my life. Joining the Rangers isn't one of them. She isn't either." It didn't matter that she had secrets; he knew how she felt or they couldn't have shared what they had.

Sly nodded toward the door. The two of them strode out onto the LCAC's deck. Everything was dark now except for a small worklight in one corner. The rear ramp was down—the front was jammed against a stout pine tree barely a dozen feet tall—and Sly led him off the stern of the hovercraft and out into the night.

With no other lights shining from the LCAC or up on the hills, the stars were a solid arc across the sky. Dawn was still a several hours off. By some unspoken agreement, they stopped a hundred yards toward the beach and watched the sky together. A lone meteor slid by, otherwise the sky was motionless. There was a sharp smell of pine pitch in the sheltered cove.

"I've served three tours with her now, two of them aboard my boat," Sly's voice sounded out of the dark barely louder than the wind on the cliffs that surrounded them. The sea salt was so thick on the air that even the storm couldn't clear it away.

Clint waited him out.

"Still don't know what drives her, but I'll tell you one thing."

"What's that?" Clint asked when Sly had lapsed into a long silence.

"I've never seen her serious about a man before. There's the occasional light and casual…"

And Clint did his best to ignore the gutful of jealousy that had him clenching his chilled hands into fists when he pictured another man touching her.

"…but mostly she keeps men away. Tosses them aside hard when they try to stick."

"Uh huh." Clint didn't like that image any more than the last one.

"If you're serious, don't let her do that to you." And Sly's tone said that's all he was going to offer.

Clint was a US Ranger. He knew all about hanging tough.

Chapter 11

*W*e're done, Lieutenant," Nika held her voice steady as they strode up the beach. "It's not you. You're the best man I've ever been with. It's me. I just don't want what you do." There. She'd said it.

"Uh huh," Clint nodded comfortably. She glanced over at him and, though he was gazing ahead, she could tell that he wore that knowing half smile of his that looked so good on him, even if she did want to scrub it off with a beach cobble. "Fine day for it."

She'd slept thirteen hours on steel decking and it felt good to be out and moving around. The *Peleliu* was still six hours out, so they owned this remote corner of Gavdos Island for a while longer. No rain had reached the parched island but the wind still roared and she was glad to be wearing the Santa hat, no matter how ridiculous it must look. She just ignored the impression of Clint's warmth inside it.

Clint strode along with his hands rammed into his jacket pockets, but otherwise appeared oblivious to the chilly wind. Or her declaration that it was over between them.

It was the last hour of sunset and the sun was already blood red as it descended into the distant storm clouds that had yet to reach the island. Perhaps they never would. The sky above arced a blue so brilliant that it was possible to believe it would always be there, never changing, never marred by overcast. The tan rock and sand, looking dusty gray with age, was taking on the sunlight's red hue.

The crew of LCAC-316, along with its obstinate US Ranger stowaway, were the sole occupants of this end of the island. And Cape Tripiti was off the beaten path. Literally—path. In a final haze that she barely remembered, she'd driven the hovercraft partway up a hill—trackless except for a footpath barely wide enough for two people to walk side by side. It had left the LCAC with a very uncomfortable nose-up tilt. But there had been insufficient fuel to reliably start the engines, so they'd left it there for now.

The hills were dotted with a coarse, thorny scrub and the occasional wretched pine that survived the constant drought and the battering wind. She and Clint were headed for the Cape itself. The narrow headland reached almost a quarter mile past the beach, its great arches and flat top making it look like some Roman aqueduct carved by giants from living rock.

Clint still didn't say anything as they scaled up the couple hundred feet from the beach to the top surface.

"You don't seem surprised," she managed a relatively neutral tone, but had expected more of a reaction. Wanted one. Wanted to know she'd been important, even if they were done. Which was a little petty, after all, since she was the one ending it. But still she wanted some reaction.

They reached the top and the wind slapped at them. The point of the cape no longer protected them from the westerly winds. On the west side, the waves boomed and crashed against the ancient stone. Looking out to sea, she still couldn't quite believe that she'd flown across that.

Sly's "Well done" when she'd finally woken up this afternoon and her own aching body had told her quite how much she'd achieved. In eight years she'd never done anything quite like it. Keeping an entire MEU armed and aloft all by herself during her flight deck days would have been less exhausting. Seeing the ocean from the safety of land with her crew and her cargo intact, that was when she knew she'd really done something.

"What's for me to say?" Clint shrugged as he led the way out toward the point. "You want to end the best relationship either of us has ever had. I can't say it makes any sense, so I don't see much point arguing."

"The best relationship I ever had?"

"Uh huh."

"How would you know what the best—" then she could hear herself and stopped. It didn't help that he was right.

"Thought so," was his smug response.

"We're still done."

"You're repeating yourself, Petty Officer Maier."

She was. Dammit!

They were halfway out to the point before he spoke again. "Are you so sure of what I want?"

"Happy-ever-after dreams are written all over you, Lieutenant Barstowe. I know the type and you are so it."

"Well," he didn't deny it as he might have just a few weeks before. "If you're so sure what I want, then what do *you* want?"

# # #

Clint had moved on a dozen paces through the buffeting wind atop Cape Tripiti when he realized that Nika was no longer beside him. He turned and saw her rooted in place with her strong eyebrows indicating a furrow of concentration hidden beneath the brim of the Santa hat.

He backtracked to her, but she didn't seem to notice. He might as well be made of transparent glass for all of the attention she was paying him, though he stood right in front of her.

Happy-ever-after dreams were written all over him, huh? He didn't think they were, but if he considered the woman in front of him, maybe he understood why she thought that. Something about being right a hundred percent.

That intense concentration didn't break.

He reached out to brush a finger along her cheek.

"Don't do that!" Nika slapped his hand aside.

For the first time, he felt a small sliver of fear slide up his spine. If ever there was a woman stubborn enough to decide against their being together and sticking to it, it was this one.

"What is it that you dream of, Nika?"

When she finally looked up at him, he couldn't read the expression in her deep brown eyes. Not anger. Not loss. But neither were they blank. They were just…neutral.

"What?"

"I never had dreams of my own, Clint. I never did. I think…I think that I'm living someone else's dream." Then she stepped aside and continued past him as if he wasn't even there.

Now it was his turn to stare blankly at the rock before him. *Never had dreams?* That didn't even make any sense.

"Going to miss the sunset. Get a move on, Ranger," her call was almost lost upon the wind.

He turned and followed her out to the very end of the headland where the flat-top surface tapered, then crumbled until the last shredded edge tumbled down into the sea. Atop the last flat spot a concrete compass-rose, several feet across, had been set into the stone. It had large brass letters at the cardinal points. On the compass-rose stood a giant wooden chair weathered and beaten but still solid. Its slat back was ten feet tall and the broad seat itself was as high as Nika's shoulders.

Without really thinking about it, he wrapped his hands about her waist and lifted her onto the seat.

"Putting me on a pedestal, Ranger?" She swung her feet back and forth like a little kid.

He didn't bother to answer.

"From up here, I can see all of Europe."

While that was untrue—for much of the horizon was blocked by the gray bulk of Gavdos Island—the seat did face north. And they were perched at the southernmost point of all of Europe. Farther south than Malta, Sicily, or even Gibraltar.

He was looking up at the woman that perhaps he did have on a pedestal, but he also knew it was a posting she deserved. Behind her lay nothing but the Libyan Sea as the stretch of the Med from Greece to those distant and hostile shores was named.

"Whose dreams are you living then, if not your own?"

# # #

Nika looked down at Clint. He stood before her high seat, no less strong, but a great deal less certain than when they'd started their walk. She was sorry for that, but there were some parts of Keila's dream she wanted no part of. Family had never worked well for her, except as something to escape.

But if anyone deserved an honest answer, Lieutenant Clint Barstowe was that man. So she looked up once again at her view of "all of Europe." A desolate island, arid with only a few tiny settlements on the far side of its inhospitable interior. Crete lay as little more than a dark smudge on the horizon.

But it didn't feel right to speak to him from up here either. Nika slid back to the ground, but unable to face him, she turned aside and spoke to the sea. She told him of Keila's death, essentially by rape. The loss of her near-sister combined with her own lack of ambition which had formed Nika's subsequent choice to step into her best friend's shoes and live her life rather than the mess that was her own.

At some point Clint wrapped his arms around her from behind and while she appreciated their warmth against the chill wind, they did nothing to abate the chill inside as she finished the story.

"I didn't join the Navy for me; I joined it for her. I do my best to fulfill the potential that she offered the world and I didn't. A potential that maybe I could have saved, and didn't. We Jews are great at acts of atonement, especially for the dead. I never really understood that before, but this is mine. That's all there is to me, Clint. A hollow shell that is all facade and happens to be named Nika Maier."

He didn't speak and Nika could feel the cold wind blowing through her as if she didn't even exist.

"You're the only one who knows that I'm not really me."

His answer was a low chuckle that stung like a lightning bolt. Then he spoke softly, "You have no clue how amazing a woman you are, Nika. Only makes me love you all the more."

She shot an elbow back, hard.

Clint, wholly unprepared for the blow, let go his hold on her and dropped to the hard stone. He managed only a faint wheeze before he tipped over from knees to curl up on the ground.

Frozen as hard as the rock and feeling as weathered as the old chair, Nika stood and stared at what she had done. She should kneel to him. Offer succor, apologize…something. But nothing came to her.

Her voice was little louder than the wind when she spoke over him.

"There is no *me* to love."

She turned and left him. Her footsteps leaving no sound, no impression on the hard stone. She had pronounced the death sentence on her own heart while standing over her best friend's grave. In the eight years since, she had found no true sign of her heart, or of Nika Maier.

But for the first time, she wondered if she'd take her heart back if she could.

# # #

Clint managed to sit back up within thirty seconds, but it was too late, Nika was gone into the gloom of the evening. The sun had disappeared into the distant storm clouds and the light was failing. He caught occasional glimpses of her. Moving away across the headland. Descending the slope to the beach. Finally he lost track of her as she walked back toward the LCAC.

He rubbed at his solar plexus. No question that was going to hurt for a while, but his body had certainly suffered plenty worse in training and in battle. Never from a lover before, but Nika was a first in so many ways.

Clint sat there as the sky darkened: cobalt blue, midnight blue, black. The first planets came out and finally the first stars. He was cold, but a Ranger learned to ignore such inconveniences. He needed some time to think.

Nika Maier.

Her he needed a lot of time to think about.

She might have reshaped herself because of her terrible loss, but she had reshaped *herself.* There was no denying the amazing woman she'd become.

Yet she did.

"Woman needs to take a good long look in the mirror," he addressed the darkness.

But she wouldn't see herself there.

"Well, Clint, you got you some choices, my man."

He could wash his hands of her and good riddance. That was attractive in several ways. He'd sworn off marriage and heavy-duty relationships, after all. He knew he had because he'd been there when he'd done it.

Problem with knowing the why behind Nika's choice was that it only made her all the more attractive. There was an integrity inside her that went deeper than any Ranger he'd ever served with.

Option two: finding some way back to being just lovers. He'd lay another two year's pay that would end up with him right where he was at the moment—knocked on his butt and wondering what the hell had just happened.

So, that was a no-win scenario. A Ranger knew that someday there just might be a battle where you had to die to win and they trained for that as well as they could. But this was a battle that could only be won if he came out the other side of it alive.

Or…

That was the problem. He didn't know if he wanted that particular "or."

Option three: he could find a tactic that would lead them ahead until they were walking along a shared path. No question about the kind of path that would have to be with Nika Maier. With her it would have to be a path that led to: until death do us part. She was a serious kind of woman after all.

It was nuts, but his instincts also told him it was the only choice.

It would be a hell of a struggle, but he was used to that too.

He considered the battle plan. For a starter, he appeared to have Michael's and Sly's consent to proceed. No two men knew him better. But they weren't really assets in this operation, should he choose to undertake it; more like interested observers.

Other assets and liabilities? Nika associated with very few people outside the hovercraft crew and he'd wager that all of them would be solidly on her side, no matter what that was. Perhaps he could enlist the help of a few of the female Night Stalkers. On the other hand, that was a scary wildcard—no man controlled those amazing women. Married them, yes. Controlled them, not so much.

There were some missions that had difficult strategies with complex timings carefully coordinated across all units involved in the operation. It didn't take much for a battle to grow sufficiently to require a dedicated comm operator, which then meant there had to be a backup plus additional protection. In such dynamic scenarios, it required detailed planning and an exceptional team to achieve the desired goal.

Then Clint pictured the rifle practice they'd held two weeks ago aboard the *Peleliu*.

There was another approach. The lone gunman. Perhaps with a spotter, but perhaps not.

Such a strategy provided maximum flexibility and all it really required was an unearthly amount of patience. A sniper might take days to slither into position. They'd stop drinking water so that they didn't have to urinate and risk leaving any odor. Go without food, because to slip out an energy bar was to make an unnecessary motion that could be spotted.

Flexibility and patience. He had both of those down.

Clint stood and let the wind gusts slap the limestone dust off his clothes.

The stars shone brilliantly above, bright enough that he didn't need to pull a flashlight out of his thigh pocket to see his way. It lay clear before him.

"Last question. Do you really want this or do you just want the victory of achieving the goal?" It was a question a Ranger had to ask constantly. They were a very goal-driven unit by design and had to temper that with at least some common sense.

In the quest to win Nika Maier, there wasn't a whole lot of common sense involved. For once, she'd made her feelings pretty damn clear. And his main opponent in the whole effort would be Nika herself.

But there was nothing in his past like her quick laugh, her slow smile, or the amazing way she felt in his arms.

He didn't just want all that; he needed it.

"Well, Mama. You made your choices," he looked up and hoped that she was looking at the same stars, or would be when darkness reached Little Rock. "Looks like mine are down a different path."

He turned for the hovercraft.

"Hoo-ah," he told the night as he set out on his newest mission.

Three steps later he caught his boot heel on a shadowed ripple in the rock and tumbled into a sticker bush before he could catch himself.

He used the flashlight to complete the rest of Phase One of his plan…getting back to the hovercraft in one piece.

Chapter 12

They'd had to refuel from the air again, despite the dangers.

Nika felt bad about that. The night before she'd run them far enough up the lone goat path that the helo couldn't land beside them due to the slope. They'd tried restarting the engines, so that she could move down to the level beach. That effort had failed before the engines were even up to operating temperature—they ran the fuel tanks dry. Minutes. They'd made it out of the storm with just minutes to spare.

So, Captain Roberts' big twin-rotor Chinook once again hovered overhead and dumped fuel down a dangling hose. At least this time they weren't battling waves and the storm. The way the wind curled around the cape was giving the pilot some troubles, but he was a Night Stalker, so they managed.

Clint had been decent through the whole thing. He'd greeted her civilly enough on his return for nothing to seem out of place. He could have made an ugly scene, but he was too decent a guy to do that.

She certainly hoped that the two nasty scratches on his cheek weren't somehow her fault.

He did a better job of behaving normally than she managed. Every time they brushed by one another, on the deck or in the narrow confines of the hovercraft's interior spaces, she could feel her cheeks flaring with heat.

It might be okay if it had only been embarrassment at the way she'd hit him and left him.

As she waited for Dave to once again bring the engines up to temperature, she still wasn't sure what had come over her. A man had said he loved her and her reflex response was to level him.

There was also a second heat that occurred every time they passed. But, she admonished her body harshly, that one *would* be fading with time.

"At operating temperature, Craftmaster Maier," Dave informed her over the intercom.

"Clear for operations," Tom stated. "*Peleliu* now standing two miles out in the lee of the island." Downwind of the island, the wave action would be milder for several miles, making reboarding the LCAC into the Well Deck a more manageable task.

"I'm looking at a pine tree," Sly reported from the Loadmaster's portside spotter position.

"Real helpful, boss."

"Always glad to be." He'd also insisted that since she'd been the one to fly them off the *Peleliu*, it was up to her to make sure she returned his craft in one piece to where it belonged.

"Ready."

Nika barely resisted turning to look at Clint. He sat, as he had through much of the previous night, close behind Dave in the Troop Commander's seat. His was…not for her to think about any longer.

"Take us up, Tom."

As soon as he did, gravity had them slipping backwards down the slope. She made small corrections, twisting the stern side to side so as not to create a new damage path in addition to the one she'd made coming in. A winter storm from the east should erase the worst of it. By January there'd be no evidence that the US military had occupied a tiny corner of Greece in a "hostile takeover."

In moments, she was sliding backwards over the tiny salt sea—the saline lagoon she barely recalled flying over last night. With a twist of the controls, she managed to spin the hovercraft one-eighty around though the pool was only twice the LCAC's length.

When she drove out over the beach and plunged back into the surf, it felt as if her world was coming back to normal. A slash of spray had Dave reaching for the windshield wipers, Tom was calling out a heading, Sly reported all secure from the Loadmaster's station. The hovercraft felt far less like an adventure than it had yesterday. Not that it was any less fun to fly, but she'd crossed some threshold fighting that storm and now she could anticipate the motion rather than just react. She had time to think about the wind currents swirling around the cape and ease back on the wheel just before they caught and tried to spin her craft.

The *Peleliu* lay less than five minutes away at a comfortable pace. And with a thousand gallons of fuel aboard, there was no edge of panic like last night.

The ship had turned bow into the wind, so she swung wide and was able to slide up the steel beach of the rear loading ramp while in the ship's wind shadow as well as the island's.

Up the length of the Well Deck, the engines once again an outrageously loud but familiar reverberating roar on the final approach inside the ship.

She gave the command to settle the LCAC and secure from operations.

She was home.

Nika pulled off her helmet. She had to find something civil to say to Clint for all he'd done and put up with over the last thirty hours, but he was no longer in his seat. Only the spare headset, dangling on its hook, still swung back and forth to indicate he'd ever been there.

Chapter 13

T *hree days later, Clint* knew he'd miscalculated and needed some help after all. Some egotistical part of him had thought that if he stayed away, maybe Nika would change her mind and want to try again.

Now he knew that he'd grossly underestimated one of two things.

First, the strength of their mutual attraction. However, with the maddeningly sleepless nights he was experiencing himself, he didn't think that was the issue. The attraction was as real as ever and he was sure it was mutual.

Second, he'd underestimated Nika's strength of resolve that they were done. *That,* he decided, *was a serious miscalculation.*

When a man needed reinforcements on an operation there were several ways to get them. First off he'd ask. If that didn't work, he'd try shame.

"Hey, Sly," Clint caught up with the Chief just as he was heading into the weight room. He made it look like simple chance, even though he'd been lurking in wait for over half an hour.

It was an odd time of day, which is why it had taken Clint a couple forays to track down the chief for ambush. Then he'd remembered that Gail Stowell was Chief Steward aboard the ship and would be awake and in the galley hours before breakfast service began. Being a good husband, Sly would get up with her and then have a few hours to kill before it was time to eat. There was one surefire way to kill time aboard a ship at sea, pump some iron.

Clint felt pretty pleased that it had worked and he'd caught Sly alone. And it wasn't as if he'd be getting any sleep himself; there was only so much tossing and turning a man could do before giving up in total disgust.

"You're up early," Sly greeted him easily. "Thought you and my petty officer would be—" The chief grimaced. "Sorry, not my place."

Clint merely offered a disappointed grunt as he started some warm-up stretches.

Sly began his own stretches.

Clint waited until they'd each done a couple of stations, matching pound for pound and total reps without trading a word about it. When he moved to the bench, Sly moved into the spotter position. Clint loaded heavy and pushed hard, building up steam until his arms burned and his breath was coming in painful gasps. He barely managed to place the bar back on the hooks without assistance.

Sly matched him in weight, but struggled out three more reps than Clint had. He could see what it cost Sly to beat a US Ranger though and didn't feel too bad about being beaten. Not *too* bad.

Maybe if he'd slept more than a few hours in…

Clint dropped to sit on the next bench over as Sly sat up and mopped his face with his towel.

"You going to unstick your craw, or do I have to keep proving that Navy can outdo Army without even breaking a sweat?" Sly mopped at his face again.

Clint wasn't sure where to begin, "What you said before?"

Sly nodded for him to continue.

"She did it. Cast me aside."

"Shit! Sorry brother, that's got to hurt."

That didn't cover half of it. But, "Rangers don't throw in the towel that easily."

Sly's nod was encouraging this time.

"She—" and then he stopped. Nika had said that she'd never told anyone else about her past and her motivations for joining the Navy. That was precious and he couldn't betray that confidence.

He mopped at the sweat that wasn't entirely from the workout and tried again.

"I can't breathe right without her. But she's got this iron resolve."

"Might have noticed that. Might be why I recruited her from the Flight Deck." Sly picked up a dumbbell and began doing curls, but Clint could tell his mind wasn't really on it—it was just a twenty-five pounder.

"If staying away makes the heart grow fonder, it sure as hell hasn't worked."

"At least not on her," Sly said with far too much perception.

"Yeah." Clint picked up a forty and began curls of his own. It had worked entirely too well on him; he'd go mad if he couldn't find a way to get Nika back.

"So now you're bringing your sorry mess to the Navy to clean it up for you?" Sly picked up a second twenty-five and began working both arms.

"No," time to try for the shame, "I'm asking my service brother—who I stood best man for—whether or not he wants a chance to return the favor."

Sly looked up from his weights for the first time.

Clint found a second forty-pounder even though his right arm was already feeling it.

"You that serious?"

Was he? If Nika had made a different choice, would he have been willing to go down on one knee out on the windy headland at Cape Tripiti?

His mama had raised two kids and worked her way from nurse to senior administrator at the biggest hospital in Little Rock. Clint knew she'd taken a lover—he'd introduced them after all—but always a step back; always referred to as "just a friend." It worked for them.

It didn't work for him. Not when the woman was Nika Maier. Clint rose, tossed the pair of forties back on rack with clang, then faced Sly squarely.

"Yeah, Sly. I'm that serious."

Sly came over and dropped the twenty-fives into place, then slapped him on the shoulder. "Guess we better do something about it then, Clint. Because it's a guarantee that this is one time the Army is definitely going to need the Navy's aid."

"So what's our first move?"

Sly smiled. "We definitely need to recruit one more person."

"Got someone in mind?" His friend's tone was giving him hope, something that had eluded Clint for the last day or so.

"Oh yeah."

"Who?"

"Someone way smarter than the two of us put together."

"Colonel Gibson? Don't know that I really want to get Michael involved in all this." Frankly it would embarrass the hell out of him to ask.

"Nope," Sly shook his head. "Way smarter than Michael."

# # #

Thankfully Nika didn't believe in running away from problems, or she would have gone looking for a way off the ship—fast—rather than working her way down the evening chow line as if this was just a normal end of shift. Another six months remained on her current tour, so a transfer wasn't going to happen anyway. Besides, putting in for a transfer to get away from Clint Barstowe was a pansy-ass maneuver.

It wasn't as if she'd seen him in days. Nika supposed that if she'd really wanted to, it would have been easy enough to arrange. With the light crew aboard the *Peleliu,* several rules had been relaxed. She could just as easily have eaten up in the Officers Mess as she did here in the Chiefs Mess and been assured of running into him there.

Once she'd caught a glimpse of Clint during an operation. But while he'd sat in the LCAC's control station in the Troop Commander's seat, she'd been relegated back to her tiny Loadmaster's aerie on the portside; Sly was again taking his Craftmaster role. Other than that, their paths hadn't crossed once in the last four days.

She wanted to return his Santa hat. Somehow it didn't seem right for him not to be wearing it with only a day left until Christmas. But she'd still been wearing it for warmth in the cold winds on Gavdos Island when she'd walked away from him.

A part of her wished she could go back to that cove.

It had been pristine and primitive, practically an undiscovered land. She could have pulled an ensign flag out of the LCAC's storage locker and declared the land as a new discovery in the name of the good ship *Peleliu.* There had been no sign of habitation in the cove to deny her claim other than the narrow foot trail.

If she did that, she could have declared many things. Perhaps, in a new country she could have become a different person. But that didn't work aboard the *Peleliu.* As soon as she'd parked the hovercraft back belowdecks, it was as if a giant reset switch had been thrown.

Nika was here now just as she had been for most of six years. Her role was defined. Her goals were simple—one of the things she liked best about military service. Her job as Loadmaster had one hundred and thirty-seven specific operational tasks; one-ninety when she was acting as the Craftmaster. She had memorized the procedures of those tasks, as well as the ones for Tom's, Dave's, and Jerome's responsibilities; after all, the Craftmaster must be trained in and oversee all of the others. Work hard and perform to the best of her abilities and everything would be—

"Get the lead out, Maier," Tom gave her a nudge from behind. "You're blocking the lasagna."

She started to move off, saw that she hadn't taken any entrée for herself and actually collided with Tom when she doubled back to get some. Gail Stowell's lasagna was not a thing to miss.

"Where's your head at, Maier?"

That was a question she absolutely wasn't going to be answering.

She took her tray over to their usual table. Wall Rudolph was looking sad. His nose had evolved over time to be as ever changing as when it blinked on a snowy night. The nose cone of the Hellfire missile had been replaced by many objects since. It started with a red-painted drink coaster—which had gone through a startling series of color changes—before a worn Army boot heel had finally replaced it. The longest lasting—of which Nika was fairly proud—was a blinking button she'd fabricated that proclaimed "Girl reindeer lead the way." But without Clint there to see it, the joke didn't really work and she was relieved when it had then turned into a circular cutout of a Monet water lilies postcard, then a split corn muffin that looked like a tiny elf mooning them, and then…

She sat next to Jerome and wondered how so much food had ended up on her plate; she wouldn't be getting through half of it.

"Pretty crappy happy face there, Maier. Christmas Eve tomorrow," Sly plunked his tray down directly across from her.

"Asshole," she muttered but only loudly enough for herself to hear. He was right of course and it was time she cured that. This time she said it aloud and backed it up with a bit of sass, "Asshole."

"Been called worse," Sly admitted happily enough.

"What are you looking so damn pleased about?"

"Me?" Sly went for an I'm-so-innocent look that she wasn't buying in the least. "Nothing. Nothing at all."

"Which is a crock of crap."

"Hey, show some respect for the badge," he tugged on his t-shirt sleeve where his uniform's badge would have been if he'd been wearing one.

"A *total* crock of crap, Chief."

"How's the lasagna?" Chief Steward Gail Stowell came up to their table and wrapped an arm around her husband's shoulder, planting a kiss atop his head. Perfect setup to put Sly in his place.

"You know that your husband puts ketchup on all your meals when you aren't looking? Here, let me help," Nika grabbed a squeeze bottle from the end of the table and fired a stream onto Sly's serving even as he protested.

He grabbed for the mustard bottle, but Gail slapped his hand as if he was a two-year old, not a twenty-year veteran.

"Would you like to come eat with me?"

"And how," Nika was up with her tray before Gail could second guess her offer. There was a friendly courtesy that emanated from the Chief Steward, but it might be the first time it had ever been extended directly to Nika. She felt a little like a happy girl following in a fairy godmother's wake. Gail led her back into the Main Galley which lay just aft of the Chiefs Mess.

Nika was completely taken aback by what she found there.

She'd been in the kitchen a few times before with Sly. His wife ran an immaculate kitchen filled with gleaming steel surfaces and giant kitchen machines invariably painted Navy gray. They had mixing bowls big enough for Nika to fit right in, and massive whisks far bigger than her head.

She'd always admired how thoroughly Gail belonged here. She looked so smooth and sophisticated in her immaculate chef whites. Her dark hair down fell in a neat, short ponytail that only added to the image. She looked almost as beautiful here in her kitchen as she had in her wedding dress.

Nika briefly wondered what it was like to be that way, but discarded the notion quickly. Gail was tall, thoughtlessly elegant, and a two-time winner of the coveted Admiral Ney award for best mess in her class of ship. Nika was—in a rare moment of self-consciousness—on the verge of retreating before she crossed the threshold.

And as she crossed the threshold, she wished she had run while she had the chance. In the background, the kitchen was still in full swing. The final trays of lasagna, innumerable loaves of garlic bread, and massive bowls of salad were being finished and delivered. The dishwashing station was barely controlled mayhem.

But there was also a secondary operation going on. The staff no longer needed on the cook line were starting on what could only be Christmas Eve dinner. There was a whole line of turkeys being dressed. Great mounds of bread cubes and chestnuts overshadowed by the savory smell of frying sausage spoke of the amazing stuffing that would be served with the birds.

None of that was daunting, though the scale of the operation was damned impressive.

No, it was the group around central stainless steel prep table that was setting Nika back on her heels.

"I needed some extra hands," Gail said lightly as if Nika wasn't facing the most daunting collection of women imaginable.

It was the three Night Stalker pilots: Lola, Trisha, and Claudia. The team leader from New Orleans who should have been a magazine model with her dark flow of curling hair and her dusky skin. The fiery-haired Little Bird pilot from Boston. And the near silent but powerful and brilliantly blond woman who had married Michael Gibson—the best soldier of them all. Only Kara Moretti, the Brooklyn Italian drone pilot was missing, probably flying some surveillance mission.

They were all dressed in standard shipboard wear of camo pants and black t-shirts that only showed off their soldier-fit physiques. Over that, white aprons which made them look uniformly girded for battle.

On the table before them were spread all of the makings for Christmas cookies.

# # #

"Something feels wrong, brother." Clint knew he was being an antsy idiot, but he couldn't stop himself. As soon as the coast was clear, Sly had slipped up to the Officers Mess to fill him in on progress.

"What do you mean?" Sly sounded offended. "It went off exactly as planned."

"I've learned that around Nika, *nothing* goes off exactly as planned."

At least Sly had the decency to sober up a bit at that comment. Then he brightened and slapped Clint's shoulder hard enough that he was knocked into Michael who sat beside him.

"She's in Gail's hands. What could possibly go wrong?"

Clint felt a little better. Gail was an amazing woman after all and she had agreed readily enough to help him out. Then Clint made a mistake and looked at Michael.

There was a speculative look on Michael's features as he turned back to his meal. He offered the tiniest nod toward an empty table near the center of the mess.

It took Clint a moment to recall who typically sat there, then he saw it in his mind's eye—the women of the Night Stalkers. If there was ever a group of women to reckon with, they were it. And if they weren't here, then they were—

Clint's nerves roared back to life.

# # #

"You know this was a setup, right?"

"I don't need any signposts to figure that out," Nika managed to respond to Gail, though she was still unable to move from the galley's threshold. Courtesy was all that held her in place against the sound tactic of beating a hasty retreat.

"Well, I've got news for you," Gail's voice remained calm and polite as if she knew how close Nika was to running. "Just don't tell our menfolk."

"What's that?" Cookie production had stopped and all four of the women were looking at her as she stood like a mannequin clutching her tray of untouched food.

"We are completely on your side, not theirs. So, no pressure from us."

Nika carefully checked the others' eyes and saw that Gail had spoken nothing but truth.

At Nika's tentative smile, Trisha piped up, "Wouldn't that surprise the shit out of them? Just imagine. *Lysistrata.* Joan of Arc. One of those things. We take over and the men will never know what happened to them."

"I thought we already had taken over," Lola turned back to rolling out the dough in front of her.

"Yes," Claudia observed in her soft voice. "But they have yet to realize that we did."

"Men really are so sweet," Trisha took a big fingerful of icing off her mixing spoon and stuffed it into her mouth. "Yum!" And her tone made it clear that she wasn't talking about the icing.

"Sit," Gail waved to a small clear spot at the end of the table. "Eat."

"Sure," Trisha spoke around her mouthful of icing. "We'll wait until after you've finished your dinner before we start dissecting your soul."

Nika could do without that, but decided that she was way past having a choice. Besides, there was a we're-all-in-it-together here even tighter than Sly's handpicked crew and she could already feel its warmth.

"Fine," she set her tray down and dragged out a high stool from under the table. "You want to dissect souls? You first, Trisha."

"Don't have one. They're too messy. I just have sugar and sweetness inside," and her smile was both sloppy with icing and absolutely genuine.

Nika poked a fork into the lasagna and tasted it. It *was* damned good. Too bad Sly had ketchup all over it.

# # #

Clint moved quietly as he scouted ahead. Quick eye check through a doorway, then roll back out of sight while his mind processed what his eyes had seen.

Clear, no noteworthy activity. A few groups seated at tables. Finished meals pushed aside.

Choosing the cover of a distant clatter of sound, he slipped past the doorway and continued down the passageway. A brief commotion ahead masked any sound of his footsteps and he used the distraction to travel more rapidly to the next doorway.

Just shy of the frame, he once against became still. A burst of laughter punctuated by a sharp bang of steel.

He knew that the human eye was more alert to motion at normal head level, so he squatted and did a roll-in, roll-out one-eyed check through this door at knee height.

One, two, three, four...five in a close group, exactly as expected. Beyond them, others in the motion.

One seated. Back to the door. A back he would know anywhere whether in a tight Navy blue t-shirt as it presently was, naked before him as it had sometimes been, or wrapped in full service gear while flying a hovercraft. And if he'd needed further proof, she had a Santa hat sticking out of her back pocket.

That he would take as an encouraging sign.

He continued squatting in the corridor outside the *Peleliu's* main galley, his back resting against the steel bulkhead and listened. No distinguishable words, but a tone of light banter and easy laughs. Women's voices overlapped rapidly in multiple cascading conversations that were impossible to follow. How did they do that?

Then a voice stood out, the excited tones of Trisha O'Malley.

"Just stretch him out on the table here and we'll cut him down to size for you," followed by the sharp whack of a knife landing hard against a cutting board.

That didn't sound good.

A round of laughter following.

Really not good. His instincts, as confirmed by Michael, were right; things were getting out of hand.

He closed his eyes for a moment and sighed. He needed a new plan and he needed it fast.

"Try it, you'll like it," Trisha's voice again cutting through the general noise from inside the galley.

Try what? Oh. His mind sorted out the rest of the image that his quick glance had captured. He'd been overwhelmed by the sight of Nika. But now he could see what she'd been doing, what all of the women had been doing.

Making Christmas cookies.

Well, if he ever needed a new plan of attack, that was one holiday custom made to his liking.

He twisted back to his feet and hurried back up a ladderway. If the gods of Christmas cheer were still with him, he'd catch Sly and Michael before they cleared out of the mess.

Chapter 14

Trisha had handed her a baked gingerbread man on which she'd piped a particularly large bulge of icing between his legs.

"Tried it already," Nika said back to her. "Like it just fine." She bit the head off the cookie and mimicked Trisha's earlier "Yum" sound to make her point, evoking another round of laughter. Nika couldn't remember the last time she'd laughed so much.

"Den wha' be de problem, gel?" Lola asked in a New Orleans Creole accent so thick it might have been spoken by some ancient voodoo-priestess crone.

That sobered Nika. There were things she'd explained to Clint, that she still couldn't believe that she'd told him, but she definitely wasn't going to be explaining to anyone else. However, her new friends deserved an answer.

Friends. Impossibly, in just a few hours of making cookies, she knew they were. Nika hadn't collected many friends over the years. People she served with, respected, liked, even hung

out with. But this circle of women was different. They were…
friends. No other word fit.

As the rest of the kitchen staff had come off meal duty, they'd
shifted over to cookie prep, rolling out the big sheets of light
sugar dough and dark gingerbread, and then punching down the
cookie cutouts and doing the baking. Their table had switched
over to focusing completely on the decorating. Piping bags of
royal icing in a half dozen colors lay about the table. Bowls of
cinnamon hearts, bright sprinkles, and *nonpareil* balls. There
was even a supply of those white and silver sugar pearls that
were harder than jacketed bullets.

Trisha, for all the chaos that seemed to surround her, had
the finest hand for decoration other than Gail. Claudia was
also neat and precise. Lola was somewhat more chaotic, but
her imagination made for fantastic, if unexpected results.
Nika had been relegated to piping a neat line around the
edges of cookies and then filling in the inside space with
a lighter float of royal icing, leaving it for others to create
the details. The few that she had done to completion on
her own had been deemed acceptable only for immediate
consumption.

"I didn't realize that cookie decoration was such a learned
skill." She'd never decorated a Christmas cookie in her life. Mom
didn't believe in baking; she believed in store-bought and, when
there was an important social event, catering.

"Stick with us," Gail decorated another half-dozen cookies
with an effortless flourish. "You'll get the hang of it."

"Yes, ma'am," she did her best to imitate Lola's earlier crone.
"Whatever youse says, ma'am," which earned her the laugh she'd
been seeking.

Except from Claudia. Claudia Gibson set down her piping
bag and turned to look at her.

In that moment Nika knew she was screwed. She could fend
off Trisha with a tease and Lola with a laugh. She'd found she
could even dodge Gail because she had too much Southern

politeness to push. But Claudia's frank gaze wasn't going to let her squirm aside or deny who she was.

"I—" Nika tried to answer her, but couldn't find the words. The rest of the activity around the table eased to a halt. The others in the kitchen blurred into the background until she could barely see them.

Somehow the four women had all been waiting for this. Had simply been waiting for her to reach a point where…where she couldn't speak.

Not a one of them, not even Trisha, had a laugh for her, or even a smile.

It was Claudia who broke the silence. "There's a moment, isn't there? A moment when the way forward is as clouded as the way back."

Nika could only nod. They'd teased her about Clint with an easy way, with a fair dose of lewd jokes. They'd regaled her and each other with tales of their own husbands—both the good and the bad—but there was no denying their deep love for their men. It was a sound that had pulled and tugged at her until now she sat in the midst of their quiet circle and didn't know what to say.

"He's the best man I've ever met." The others nodded soberly.

"In or out of bed?" Trisha teased and Lola just rolled her eyes at her friend's back.

"Both." And Nika knew it was true as soon as she'd said it. Her body ached with its need for him. But that wasn't the best of him. It was the man who cared for his troops, for the women he'd rescued, and for herself that had been literally swept her off her feet.

She had abused him and dumped him, and he hadn't thrown it back in her face as any other man would have. What had he done instead? He'd recruited Gail to find some way to win her back. An interesting choice, one of blind faith. He'd have no control over how his tactic fared, but he had taken the risk anyway. That's when she understood even more of him. He wasn't going to give up; he didn't know the meaning of the word.

Instead he'd said that he loved her. Even more, he'd said it after she'd told him that it wasn't her life she was living. He saw her as stronger for having followed the path she had walked, not weaker.

And she *was* the one who had walked it, not her best friend. She was an LCAC Loadmaster on a ship that catered to the most elite Special Operations team she'd ever seen or heard of: Night Stalkers, Delta's senior warrior, and Clint's Rangers combined.

She was a Craftmaster-in-training. *Not* Keila. All the things she'd done in her best friend's name were also hers.

Nika hadn't seen that. But…

But Clint had. And she'd…Oh god, she'd cast him aside.

"Think she's ready for it?" Trisha asked.

Nika couldn't look up, just stared down at the table in front of her. She wasn't ready for anything.

Claudia slipped a cookie in front of her. For a moment Nika wondered why, because it was already finished.

And it was awful.

Not even up to her own lame standard. The edges were all crooked, the piping wiggled in ridiculous fashion, and the icing was battleship gray and black—no one in their right mind would eat this cookie.

Then she focused on it.

It was an LCAC.

The edges weren't made with a cookie cutter; this was a knife-cookie, carved out of a sheet of dough by an inexpert hand. The profile was head-on and two large fans humped the top of the cookie. The black rubber spray skirt was a smear of black across the bottom and the rest a smudgy version of *Navy-gray* icing. A control station and Loadmaster's station had been piped into place with some care and an unpracticed hand. Red and green *nonpareils* had been very carefully placed between the two stations, like a drooping line of Christmas lights.

In the center of the cookie, roughly mid-deck, had been placed a pair of cinnamon hearts.

Only one hand could have made this and the thoughtfulness behind it had her wiping at her eyes. Clint had chosen *her* place to make the cookie. He knew where she belonged, even if she didn't. Hadn't.

"Oh god," she blinked hard and had to wipe her eyes again before she could see the women standing with her. She could see that they were in on it. Could now recall Claudia leaving at odd moments, perhaps meeting with Clint out in the hall.

But she could also see that they weren't plotting against her. There wasn't a dry eye among them, they were all four...all five counting herself...a complete mess.

Gail handed her a paper napkin that she used to daub her eyes and then blow her nose.

"Where is he?"

But she knew even before she asked.

Careful not to break it, she placed Clint's butt-ugly beautiful LCAC cookie on a fresh napkin and headed out to find him.

Chapter 15

Nika knew where she was going, but still wasn't prepared for what she found there.

The *Peleliu's* Well Deck was deserted. The LCAC sat there with its bow ramp raised, still looking like a murdered steel shoebox. The only light in the whole cavernous space came from red-and-green Christmas lights that had indeed been strung between the two control stations. It looked just like the cookie she still cradled carefully in both of her hands.

With a sharp hiss that made her jump, the bow ramp released and then folded open before her. She had started to look up toward the shadowed control station. Instead her eyes were riveted to what was revealed as the ramp lowered.

Sitting in the center of the deck stood a two-foot tall Christmas tree. When she boarded and moved closer, she could see its details. The tree was formed from two plates of eighth-inch steel hastily cut with a welding torch, rejoined in tree shape, and painted bright green. It too had been draped with lights—white ones that twinkled on and off. Ornaments had been stuck on all over its surfaces—the many incarnations of Rudolph's nose, each saved as if for this moment. Even her "Girl reindeer lead the way" button blinked on and off from its place of honor near the very top. The tree had been crowned with a steel star—a six-pointed Star of David. He'd made her a Hanukkah bush.

A blanket had been spread before the tree. At the center stood an ammo can for 7.62mm rounds with the lid flopped open and a bouquet of roses cut from the red cloth warning covers used to protect missiles prior to loading onto aircraft. A small picnic had been set up before it: a small basket of some of Gail's finest cookies, a bottle of cider, two glasses. She set Clint's cookie in the basket.

She felt rather than heard the man moving toward her out of the hatch from the control station ladder. Nika rose to her feet, but didn't turn as she waited for him.

He stopped a mere step behind her.

Nika tried to speak, but completely failed past the tightness in her throat.

Clint finally saved her, "I see you got my cookie."

She nodded quickly, "Most beautiful one I ever saw." And she looked back down at it, knowing she'd start crying again if she turned to look at him. And that's when the two hearts registered. Really registered. Clint had placed them as closely together as the two of them now stood. "Truly Clint, you're the best man I've ever known."

"Despite leveling me on the dirt?"

"I wish we could go back there, to that cove. Redo the past and make it our cove. Redo so much of the past." But would she? The cove, yes. But somehow, as if it was woman's magic, the circle of incredible, cookie-baking women, had made her see that whatever road she might have traveled, it had led *her*, Nika Maier, here. In the present tense, here seemed like a good place to be—a very good place.

"How about redoing the future?" Clint's voice was light, but she could hear the weight behind it. She knew his every tone and the question was desperately important to him.

She turned to look up at him, his dark features lit by the blinking Hanukkah bush lights behind her. "Can't redo something that hasn't been done yet, Ranger."

His smile reflected some of his relief. "I don't know, sailor. I was picturing a future without you and it wasn't working so good in my brain."

"Well, it is just an Army brain, soldier. I wouldn't expect too much of it."

Clint's smile remained, but it turned serious despite the lightness he kept in his tone, "This man's Army brain knows what it wants, Navy. Does yours?"

Nika thought about it. Did she? She'd lived someone else's dreams for the last eight years of her life. It was a surprise gift that they had become her own without her noticing. But maybe it was time to start living dreams that were completely her own. More than maybe.

"It might, Army. My brain has some definite ideas."

He brushed a finger down her cheek and she could see that Clint knew what it had cost her, both the past and owning the present. He knew her like no one else ever had, not even herself. No more doubts remained of what she wanted for the future. His question was so in sync with her feelings that it came as no surprise when he asked it.

"So, what do you think, Maier? In the mood to make a promise?"

"Nope," she couldn't make it that easy on him. "Sorry to disappoint you, Lieutenant."

She saw him take it in. It was a bitter pill, but he swallowed it down quickly and the look of absolute determination came once more into his eyes. Nika had been right; there was no stopping a Ranger once he'd set his sights on something. And with a heart like Clint's behind that determination, a woman couldn't ask for more.

"However," she moved a half step closer and rested a hand on his chest. She could feel the shiver of relief that rippled up his frame. "I might be in the mood to break one."

"I think you'll have to explain that, Petty Officer. Remember, I'm just a simple Army Ranger. We like to have things spelled out for us, especially when they don't make any damned sense at all."

"I made a promise to myself. I have never once broken such a promise. For you I just might make this one time exception."

"Be okay if I ask what that promise is?" He slid his hands onto her waist and she allowed him to drag her slowly in until they were pressed together and her nose once more rested against the center of his chest.

"I promised myself I would never fall in love."

"Huh. Well, I wouldn't want you to be breaking any promises on my account." He kissed her on top of her head and it warmed her all the way through.

She tilted her head back to smile up at him, "I think we're too late for that, Ranger." She pulled the Santa hat out of her back pocket and tugged it on his head. Then she let her hands rest on his shoulders. "But I'll tell you what."

"What?" He twisted his head to flip the pom-pom to the back. "You've only got a moment before the man in the Santa hat kisses you, woman. So speak quick."

"When we find an aisle to walk down, I'll let you lead the way."

He said only one thing before he leaned down to seal his promise with a kiss.

"Hoo-ah!"

About the Author

M. L. Buchman has over 40 novels in print. His military romantic suspense books have been named Barnes & Noble and NPR "Top 5 of the Year," nominated for the Reviewer's Choice Award for "Top 10 Romantic Suspense of 2014" by RT Book Reviews, and twice Booklist "Top 10 of the Year" placing two of his titles on their "The 101 Best Romance Novels of the Last 10 Years." In addition to romance, he also writes thrillers, fantasy, and science fiction.

In among his career as a corporate project manager he has: rebuilt and single-handed a fifty-foot sailboat, both flown and jumped out of airplanes, designed and built two houses, and bicycled solo around the world.

He is now making his living as a full-time writer on the Oregon Coast with his beloved wife. He is constantly amazed at what you can do with a degree in Geophysics. You may keep up with his writing by subscribing to his newsletter at www. mlbuchman.com.

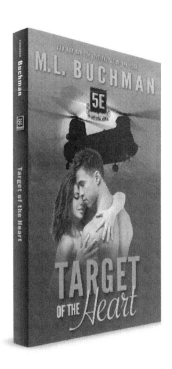

Target of the Heart
(excerpt)

—a Night Stalkers 5E Novel—

*M*ajor Pete Napier hovered his MH-47G Chinook helicopter ten kilometers outside of Lhasa, Tibet and a mere two inches off the tundra. A mixed action team of Delta Force and The Activity—the slipperiest intel group on the planet—flung themselves aboard.

The additional load sent an infinitesimal shift in the cyclic control in his right hand. The hydraulics to close the rear loading ramp hummed through the entire frame of the massive helicopter. By the time his crew chief could reach forward to slap an "all secure" signal against his shoulder, they were already ten feet up and fifty out. That was enough altitude. He kept the nose down as he clawed for speed in the thin air at eleven thousand feet.

"Totally worth it," one of the D-boys announced as soon as he was on the Chinook's internal intercom.

He'd have to remember to tell that to the two Black Hawks flying guard for him…when they were in a friendly country and could risk a radio transmission. This deep inside China—or rather Chinese-held territory as the CIA's mission-briefing spook had insisted on calling it—radios attracted attention and were only used to avoid imminent death and destruction.

"Great, now I just need to get us out of this alive."

"Do that, Pete. We'd appreciate it."

He wished to hell he had a stealth bird like the one that had gone into bin Laden's compound. But the one that had crashed during that raid had been blown up. Where there was one, there were always two, but the second had gone back into hiding as thoroughly as if it had never existed. He hadn't heard a word about it since.

The Tibetan terrain was amazing, even if all he could see of it was the monochromatic green of night vision. And blackness. The largest city in Tibet lay a mere ten kilometers away and they were flying over barren wilderness. He could crash out here and no one would know for decades unless some yak herder stumbled upon them. Or were yaks in Mongolia? He was a corn-fed, white boy from Colorado, what did he know about Tibet? Most of the countries he'd flown into on black ops missions he'd only seen at night anyway.

While moving very, very fast.

Like now.

The inside of his visor was painted with overlapping readouts. A pre-defined terrain map, the best that modern satellite imaging could build made the first layer. This wasn't some crappy, on-line, look-at-a-picture-of-your-house display. Someone had a pile of dung outside their goat pen? He could see it, tell you how high it was, and probably say if they were pygmy goats or full-size LaManchas by the size of their shit-pellets if he zoomed in.

On top of that were projected the forward-looking infrared camera images. The FLIR imaging gave him a real-time overlay, in case someone had put an addition onto their goat shed since the last satellite pass, or parked their tractor across his intended flight path.

His nervous system was paying autonomic attention to that combined landscape. He also compensated for the thin air at altitude as he instinctively chose when to start his climb over said goat shed or his swerve around it.

It was the third layer, the tactical display that had most of his attention. At least he and the two Black Hawks flying escort on him were finally on the move.

To insert this deep into Tibet, without passing over Bhutan or Nepal, they'd had to add wingtanks on the Black Hawks' hardpoints where he'd much rather have a couple banks of Hellfire missiles. Still, they had 20mm chain guns and the crew chiefs had miniguns which was some comfort.

While the action team was busy infiltrating the capital city and gathering intelligence on the particularly brutal Chinese assistant administrator, he and his crews had been squatting out in the wilderness under a camouflage net designed to make his helo look like just another god-forsaken Himalayan lump of granite.

Command had determined that it was better for the helos to wait on site through the day than risk flying out and back in. He and his crew had stood shifts on guard duty, but none of them had slept. They'd been flying together too long to have any new jokes, so they'd played a lot of cribbage. He'd long ago ruled no gambling on a mission, after a fistfight had broken out about a bluff hand that cost a Marine three hundred and forty-seven dollars. Marines hated losing to Army no matter how many times it happened. They'd had to sit on him for a long time before he calmed down.

Tonight's mission was part of an on-going campaign to discredit the Chinese "presence" in Tibet on the international stage—as if occupying the country the last sixty years didn't count toward ruling, whether invited or not. As usual, there was a crucial vote coming up at the U.N.—that, as usual, the Chinese could be guaranteed to ignore. However, the ever-hopeful CIA was in a hurry to make sure that any damaging information that they could validate was disseminated as thoroughly as possible prior to the vote.

Not his concern.

His concern was, were they going to pass over some Chinese sentry post at their top speed of a hundred and ninety-six miles an hour? The sentries would then call down a couple Shenyang J-16 jet fighters that could hustle along at Mach 2 to fry his sorry ass. He knew there was a pair of them parked at Lhasa along with some older gear that would be just as effective against his three helos.

"Don't suppose you could get a move on, Pete?"

"Eat shit, Nicolai!" He was a good man to have as a copilot. Pete knew he was holding on too tight, and Nicolai knew that a joke was the right way to ease the moment.

He, Nicolai, and the four pilots in the two Black Hawks had a long way to go tonight and he'd never make it if he stayed so tight on the controls that he could barely maneuver. Pete eased off and felt his fingers tingle with the rush of returning blood. They dove down into gorges and followed them as long as they dared. They hugged cliff walls at every opportunity to decrease their radar profile. And they climbed.

That was the true danger—they would be up near the helos' limits when they crossed over the backbone of the Himalayas in their rush for India. The air was so rarefied that they burned fuel at a prodigious rate. Their reserve didn't allow for any extended battles while crossing the border...not for any battle at all really.

#

It was pitch dark outside her helicopter when Captain Danielle Delacroix stamped on the left rudder pedal while giving the big Chinook right-directed control on the cyclic. It tipped her most of the way onto her side, but let her continue in a straight line. A Chinook's rotors were sixty feet across—front to back they overlapped to make the spread a hundred feet long. By cross-controlling her bird to tip it, she managed to execute a straight line between two mock pylons only thirty feet apart. They were made of thin cloth so they wouldn't down the helo if you sliced one—she was the only trainee to not have cut one yet.

At her current angle of attack, she took up less than a half-rotor of width, just twenty-four feet. That left her nearly three feet to either side, sufficient as she was moving at under a hundred knots.

The training instructor sitting beside her in the copilot's seat didn't react as she swooped through the training course at Fort Campbell, Kentucky. Only child of a single mother, she was used to providing her own feedback loops, so she didn't expect anything else. Those who expected outside validation rarely survived the SOAR induction testing, never mind the two years of training that followed.

As a loner kid, Danielle had learned that self-motivated congratulations and fun were much easier to come by than external ones. She'd spent innumerable hours deep in her mind as a pre-teen superheroine. At twenty-nine she was well on her way to becoming a real life one, though Helo-girl had never been a character she'd thought of in her youth.

External validation or not, after two years of training with the U.S. Army's 160th Special Operations Aviation Regiment she was ready for some action. At least *she* was convinced that she was. But the trainers of Fort Campbell, Kentucky had not signed off on anyone in her trainee class yet. Nor had they given any hint of when they might.

She ducked ten tons of racing Chinook under a bridge and bounced into a near vertical climb to clear the power line on the far side. Like a ride on the toboggan at Terrassee Dufferin during *Le Carnaval de Québec,* only with five thousand horsepower at her fingertips. Using her Army signing bonus—the first money in her life that was truly hers—to attend *Le Carnaval* had been her one trip back to her birthplace since her mother took them to America when she was ten.

To even apply to SOAR required five years of prior military rotorcraft experience. She had applied after seven years because of a chance encounter—or rather what she'd thought was a chance encounter at the time.

Captain Justin Roberts had been a top Chinook pilot, the one who had convinced her to switch from her beloved Black Hawk and try out the massive twin-rotor craft. One flight and she'd been a goner, begging her commander until he gave in and let her cross over to the new platform. Justin had made the jump from the 10th Mountain Division to the 160th SOAR not long after that.

Then one night she'd been having pizza in Watertown, New York a couple miles off the 10th's base at Fort Drum.

"Danielle?" Justin had greeted her with the surprise of finding a good friend in an unexpected place. Danielle had liked Justin—even if he was a too-tall, too-handsome cowboy and completely knew it. But "good friend" was unusual for Danielle, with anyone, and Justin came close.

"Captain Roberts," as a dry greeting over the top edge of her Suzanne Brockmann novel didn't faze him in the slightest.

"Mind if I join ya?" A question he then answered for himself by sliding into the opposite seat and taking a slice of her pizza. She been thinking of taking the leftovers back to base, but that was now an idle thought.

"Are you enjoying life in SOAR?" she did her best to appear a normal, social human, a skill she'd learned by rote. *Greeting*

someone you knew after a time apart? Ask a question about them.
"They treating you well?"

"Whoo-ee, you have no idea, Danielle," his voice was smooth as…well, always…so she wouldn't think about it also sounding like a pickup line. He was beautiful, but didn't interest her; the outgoing ones never did.

"Tell me." *Men love to talk about themselves, so let them.*

And he did. But she'd soon forgotten about her novel, and would have forgotten the pizza if he hadn't reminded her to eat.

His stories shifted from intriguing to fascinating. There was a world out there that she'd been only peripherally aware of. The Night Stalkers of the 160th SOAR weren't simply better helicopter pilots, they were the most highly-trained and best-equipped ones on the planet. Their missions were pure razor's edge and black-op dark.

He'd left her with a hundred questions and enough interest to fill out an application to the 160th. Being a decent guy, Justin even paid for the pizza after eating half.

The speed at which she was rushed into testing told her that her meeting with Justin hadn't been by chance and that she owed him more than half a pizza next time they met. She'd asked after him a couple of times since she'd made it past the qualification exams—and the examiners' brutal interviews that had left her questioning her sanity, never mind her ability.

"Justin Roberts is presently deployed, ma'am," was the only response she'd ever gotten.

Now that she was through training—almost, had to be soon, didn't it?—Danielle realized that was probably less of an evasion and more likely to do with the brutal op tempo the Night Stalkers maintained. The SOAR 1st Battalion had just won the coveted Lt. General Ellis D. Parker awards for Outstanding Combat Aviation Battalion *and* Aviation Battalion of the Year. They'd been on deployment every single day of the last year, actually of the last decade-plus since 9/11.

The very first Special Forces boots on the ground in Afghanistan were delivered that October by the Night Stalkers and nothing had slacked off since. Justin might be in the 5th battalion D company, but they were just as heavily assigned as the 1st.

Part of their training had included tours in Afghanistan. But unlike their prior deployments, these were brief, intense, and then they'd be back in the States pushing to integrate their new skills.

SOAR needed her training to end and so did she.

Danielle was ready for the job, in her own, inestimable opinion. But she wasn't going to get there until the trainers signed off that she'd reached fully mission-qualified proficiency.

The Fort Campbell training course was never set up the same from one flight to the next, but it always had a time limit. The time would be short and they didn't tell you what it was. So she drove the Chinook for all it was worth like Regina Jaquess waterskiing her way to U.S. Ski Team Female Athlete of the Year.

The Night Stalkers were a damned secretive lot, and after two years of training, she understood why. With seven years flying for the 10th, she'd thought she was good.

She'd been repeatedly lauded as one of the top pilots at Fort Drum.

The Night Stalkers had offered an education in what it really meant to fly. In the two years of training, she'd flown more hours than in the seven years prior, despite two deployments to Iraq. And spent more time in the classroom than her life-to-date accumulated flight hours.

But she was ready now. It was *très viscérale,* right down in her bones she could feel it. The Chinook was as much a part of her nervous system as breathing.

Too bad they didn't build men the way they built the big Chinooks—especially the MH-47G which were built specifically to SOAR's requirements. The aircraft were steady, trustworthy, and the most immensely powerful helicopters deployed in the U.S. Army—what more could a girl ask for? But finding a superhero man to go with her superhero helicopter was just a fantasy for a lonely teenage girl.

She dove down into a canyon and slid to a hover mere inches over the reservoir inside the thirty-second window laid out on the flight plan.

Danielle resisted a sigh. She was ready for something to happen and to happen soon.

Available now .

For more information on this and other titles, please visit www.mlbuchman.com

Other works by M. L. Buchman:

The Night Stalkers
The Night Is Mine
I Own the Dawn
Daniel's Christmas
Wait Until Dark
Frank's Independence Day
Peter's Christmas
Take Over at Midnight
Light Up the Night
Christmas at Steel Beach
Bring On the Dusk
Target of the Heart
Target Lock on Love
Christmas at Peleliu Cove

Firehawks
Pure Heat
Wildfire at Dawn
Full Blaze
Wildfire at Larch Creek
Wildfire on the Skagit
Hot Point

Delta Force
Target Engaged

Angelo's Hearth
Where Dreams are Born
Where Dreams Reside
Maria's Christmas Table
Where Dreams Unfold
Where Dreams Are Written

Dieties Anonymous
Cookbook from Hell: Reheated
Saviors 101

Thrillers
Swap Out!
One Chef!
Two Chef!

SF/F Titles
Nara
Monk's Maze

20636797R00103

Printed in Great Britain
by Amazon